A NOTE TO READERS

You won't find ten-year-old Sarah Smythe and her twelve-year-old brother John in history books or on the passenger list of the sailing ship, the *Mayflower.* Yet they are real in the sense that they represent the brave children and teens who fled with their parents from England and Holland almost four hundred years ago. In America, the "New World," the Pilgrims could worship God according to their own beliefs and without persecution.

The events are real or based on real happenings. Also real are persons such as John Carver, William Brewster, William Bradford, Captain Myles Standish, and many others who sacrificed much to make a country where people could be free.

SISTERS IN TIME

Sarah's
New World

THE MAYFLOWER ADVENTURE

COLLEEN L. REECE

BARBOUR
PUBLISHING

Sarah's
New World

© 2004 by Barbour Publishing, Inc.

ISBN 1-59310-203-8

Cover design by Lookout Design Group, Inc.

Published by Barbour Publishing, Inc., P.O. Box 719, Uhrichsville, Ohio 44683, www.barbourbooks.com

Our mission is to publish and distribute inspirational products offering exceptional value and biblical encouragement to the masses.

ecpa Member of the
Evangelical Christian
Publishers Association

Printed in United States of America.
5 4 3

CONTENTS

CHAPTER 1

Spies

Twelve-year-old John Smythe lay flat on the floor of the dark hallway. His right ear was pressed against the crack under the door to the parlor. He strained to make out what his parents' low voices were saying.

Just then, John heard footsteps running down the hall, and before he could move, hard wooden shoes ran into his side.

"Oomph!" John quickly covered his mouth to muffle the groan he couldn't hold back. Rubbing his bruised body, he shifted position and looked up at his ten-year-old sister, Sarah.

"Shh," he hissed.

Sarah clasped her hands against the long, white apron that covered her dark work dress and demanded, "John Smythe, what are you doing? If Father and Mother catch you, they'll—"

"They won't if you keep your voice down," he warned in a whisper. "I want to know what they're saying."

"You're spying!" Sarah accused. "Aren't you ever going to grow up? You're twelve years old—almost a man—not a three-year-old child to be listening at doors!"

"Can't you be quiet?" John hissed. He reached up a strong, wiry arm and pulled her down next to him. "You need to hear this, Sarah. It concerns us." Excitement filled his voice.

"I don't care," she whispered back. "It's wrong to listen in on others." Sarah started to scramble up, but her father's raised voice pinned her to the floor beside John.

"I see no help for it, Abigail. If we are to remain strong and true, we cannot stay longer in Holland."

"But William," Mother protested. "Is there no other way?"

Father spoke again. "Holland offered us a place of refuge and peace when we needed it. But now it is time to move on. Holland can never be our real home." He sounded sad.

"Was it not enough that we fled England before John and Sarah were born?" Mother cried.

John and Sarah looked at each other with concern. They rarely heard their parents disagree with each other like this.

"We've been here twelve years, William. Now you wish to uproot us again."

"We must find a country where we can worship freely, a place where our church will be safe from bad influences," Father replied.

A long silence followed. John edged closer to the door, not wanting to miss a single word. *Move? When? Where?* Surely they would not return to England, where they had been persecuted for worshiping God in their own way. News from across the water said things were no better in England now than when the first of their people had fled to Holland.

"I wonder if there is such a place this side of heaven." Mother sounded like she wanted to cry. "Where do you and the other men have in mind for us to go?"

John felt Sarah grab his arm. They both held their breath,

waiting for Father's answer.

Father's deep voice rolled out like thunder. "The New World. America."

"America!" John forgot all about the need for silence and let out a whoop of delight. He rose to his knees and grabbed Sarah's hand. "Did you hear that?"

"Shh!" Sarah ordered, but it was too late. Quick footsteps sounded from the parlor, and the door was flung open wide.

Off balance, John clutched harder at his sister's hand, but he couldn't save himself from falling. He sprawled inside the parlor, dragging Sarah with him and landing on one elbow.

"Ow!" He released his sister, blinked in the more brightly lit room, and rubbed his elbow.

Mother gasped in dismay.

"What is the meaning of this?" Father's stern voice brought John to his feet.

Glancing at his sister, John could see Sarah's face was red with shame and that she was blinking hard to keep back the tears that filled her green eyes.

"It's not her fault," John confessed. His straight, cropped, brown hair shone in the candlelight. The big brown eyes that sometimes looked innocent and at other times sparkled with mischief looked enormous. "Sarah came in and stumbled over me. I told her to stay."

He swallowed hard, stopped rubbing his sore elbow, and mumbled, "You always say Sarah is her brother's keeper. She tried to make me stop spying, but I wanted to hear."

John's heart warmed a little as he caught Sarah's grateful

look, but Father's answer took away the good feeling. "I don't find in the Bible that being a brother's keeper means joining in his mischief if he doesn't stop when warned."

Sarah stumbled to her feet and stood behind John. Together they awaited judgment. While Father and Mother loved their children, they also expected John and Sarah to obey.

"I'm disappointed in you both," Mother told them.

Sarah dug her toe into the woven rug and avoided looking at her mother's eyes that were so much like her own.

"So am I." Father sounded disapproving. "Sit down, please." He waited until they sat, facing each other. "I am particularly disappointed in you because of what lies ahead." He sighed and a shadow crossed his face. "In a short time, many of our people will be leaving Holland."

"For America," John eagerly said.

Father looked at him sternly.

John bit his lip and looked miserable.

"Most of the other families will be leaving all but their oldest children in Holland, but if your mother and I decide to go, we will want to keep our family together."

"You mean we would leave Holland forever?" Sarah twisted her hands beneath her apron and stared at her parents. "But what about all our friends? I've never lived anywhere but here in Leiden, and I don't want to leave Gretchen behind."

Father closed his eyes for a moment. "Leaving friends is never easy. When your mother and I left England and moved to Holland, we, too, had to leave the village we had grown up in. You've heard us tell you the story many times. But maybe telling you more of the details will help you understand why we may have to leave Leiden now."

"You lived in Scrooby, didn't you, Father?" John asked eagerly.

"Yes," Father replied, looking out the darkened window as if he could see his childhood home. "It was a poor English village on the Great North Road between London and Edinburgh, Scotland. The road had a big name, but it was actually a narrow dirt lane used by rich people who came to hunt red deer in Sherwood Forest."

"We lived in a simple cottage," Mother continued, "but nearby was a great manor house, surrounded by a moat. The house was so large it contained everything anyone needed, including a bakery and even a chapel. But only the people from the manor house and their guests could hunt the deer. Those of us in the village lived on porridge and bread. As a special treat, sometimes we'd get a bit of fish or meat."

"That doesn't seem fair," John interrupted. "God made the deer, didn't He? So why couldn't everyone hunt them?"

"The deer were claimed by the king, and it was against the law for poor people who needed food to hunt them," explained his father. "Anyone caught hunting or eating the king's deer was punished—some were even hanged."

"How awful!" Sarah's green eyes flashed, and she tossed her head so hard that her long brown braids bounced against her back.

"But that wasn't the worst problem we faced," her mother

added. "Because we wouldn't worship God the way King James wanted us to, we couldn't go to church. We had to meet in barns like criminals."

"Why did King James tell you how to worship God?" Sarah wanted to know.

"He said that 'kings are God's lieutenants and sit on God's throne,'" Father explained. "Everyone else had to do just what he said. We couldn't even ask questions! The king was afraid. If common people like us were allowed to choose their own church leaders and worship the way they believed God wanted them to, King James worried that they'd want to do the same thing in government. Then he wouldn't be so powerful.

"Our leaders became concerned about how we would survive. Elder Brewster, Edward Winslow, and William Bradford met secretly in a barn to discuss possible solutions."

"Didn't William Bradford become part of our group when he was only seventeen?" John asked.

"Yes, he did," Father answered. "That action angered the aunts and uncles who had brought him up—William's parents died when he was about nine. William's uncles ordered him, 'Give up this path to destruction. If you join that treasonous, despised group, the king's tax collectors will surely seize your land. You will be penniless, scorned, and driven out of the country.'

"William proudly said, 'I accept the king as ruler of the country. I pay my taxes but kneel to no man. I also choose my own way to worship God.'"

John's face glowed with pride as he thought of what

courage it had taken for seventeen-year-old William Bradford to take such a stand.

"So what happened at the meeting?" Sarah asked.

"The meeting in the barn started with prayer," Father answered. "Then Elder Brewster's voice rang out: 'Our people must suffer at the hands of the king's men no more! We have been taxed unmercifully. How can we go on living in a country where desperate persons are hanged for stealing a loaf of bread to keep their little ones from starving? We here this day are in danger of being thrown into jail for the rest of our lives. Or hanged on the gallows for daring to worship God in our own way! Thousands of the poor can find no work. They—'

"A horse neighed, and Elder Brewster stopped talking," Father said. "Heavy footsteps thudded on the hard ground outside the barn. William Bradford held up a warning hand. The wooden door slowly creaked open."

CHAPTER 2

Troublesome Times

"What happened?" John asked breathlessly.

"The door opened just enough to let in John Carver and our preacher, John Robinson," Father answered.

John and Sarah sighed with relief.

"John Robinson looked very stern," Father continued.

"But he is always kind to us," Sarah protested.

"Yes, but our leaders were facing a dangerous situation. Even being discovered meeting together could have landed them in prison for life, and John Robinson had just learned that two more of their followers had been sent to the dungeons. They were turned in by their own neighbors."

John gasped. "Couldn't you even trust the people you'd grown up with to keep you safe?"

"No," Mother said. "Girls and boys I had grown up playing with were willing to tell the king's men about our meetings."

"Our leaders decided it was too dangerous to stay in England any longer," Father said. "But even that decision brought problems. The law said that anyone leaving the country had to have permission. Because of our religious beliefs, we were considered traitors. The king would never agree to our leaving.

"But William Brewster reminded us that King James is not the final power on earth. 'The King of heaven and earth knows our needs,' he told us."

"It must have been hard to plan your escape without someone finding out about it and letting the king's men know," John observed.

"It was not only hard," Father replied, "it was impossible. On a dark night late in 1607, our group of men, women, and children slipped out of town and walked silently to a seaport called Boston on the east coast of England. At last we reached the small creek where a captain had promised to meet us. We waited for two days. Nothing happened, and we were afraid that someone would find us. Finally, on the second night, the captain appeared, let us aboard his ship, and collected his fee.

"Just when we thought that at last we were safe, someone bellowed, 'Stop where you are!' "

"I don't understand," Sarah said. "What happened?"

"The captain had betrayed us," Father told his family. "The officials loaded us all into smaller boats and took us ashore. We were robbed of everything we had and marched through the streets. Then we were locked up for a month before we were ordered back to our homes. Even time in prison, however, didn't change our minds. We were determined to be free."

"But everyone must have been watching you," John said.

"They were," Mother said. "And it wasn't until the next spring that we tried again to escape. This time it was even harder. All of us women and children were loaded on a small boat to sail down the River Ryton.

18

"Saying good-bye to our husbands and fathers was the hardest thing we'd ever done. The men and older boys disappeared into the dark and began the forty-mile walk to our secret meeting place. Then disaster struck. Our boat stuck in the mud at low tide. As day broke and people from a nearby village discovered us, they armed themselves with guns and clubs and came running toward us."

Father continued the story. "The Dutch skipper of the boat we had hired sent a dinghy to bring some of the men aboard. When he saw the mob of villagers heading toward the women and children, he panicked. He hoisted the sails, raised anchor, and sailed away!

"Those of us men who were still on shore ran to help the trapped women and children. We were arrested and hauled from place to place. The authorities didn't know what to do with us. We hadn't committed a crime, but we couldn't be sent back to our old villages because our homes had been sold."

Sarah blinked to keep back her tears. She had no idea that her parents had gone through so many hard times in England.

"Finally," Father said, "that summer we were released and sailed to Amsterdam."

"Why didn't you stay there?" Sarah asked.

"Amsterdam is a noisy city that didn't have much in common with quiet little Scrooby," answered Mother.

"And some of our group had serious arguments with each other," admitted Father. "After about a year, we moved the forty miles here to Leiden, and until recently we've been content. But our reasons for leaving Holland will have to wait for another day. It's late, so let's say our prayers and get to bed."

John opened his eyes and stared around his tiny room. He slid farther down in bed. The small amount of light in his room told him how early it was, too early even for Father and Mother to be up getting ready for the new day. Yet he felt so wide awake he knew he couldn't go back to sleep. He wondered what he could do that wouldn't wake up his parents. Father worked hard in the factory, and Mother worked at the loom. They both needed their rest.

"John, are you awake?" Sarah's voice whispered from the doorway of his room.

"Of course," he said, peering out at her over his coverlet. "Who can sleep when we may be going to America? Oh, Sarah, it's going to be wonderful!"

Sarah perched on a stool by his bed and pulled her shawl closer around her. "I just don't want to leave Leiden. It's so beautiful, and our friends are all here."

John's brown hair stood straight up from sleeping. "I'm sorry everyone won't be going, but think of what fun those who do go will have."

"I still don't understand why any of us have to leave Holland."

John awkwardly patted her hand, the way he used to do when they were both small. "There are a lot of reasons. I heard Father say—"

"You've been listening again," Sarah accused.

"Do you want me to answer your question or not?" he demanded.

"Yes, please."

"Pastor Robinson and our elders are concerned because we are getting more like the Dutch every day. We dress like them. We talk like them. I like the Dutch ways." His brown gaze bored into her green eyes. "The Dutch are fun! They laugh and dance and sing, even on the Sabbath. What is wrong with dancing and singing? God wants us to be happy, doesn't He?"

John didn't wait for an answer. "Sometimes I wish our church weren't so strict, don't you? Sarah, we aren't even allowed to smile in church, and the sermons are so long!"

Sarah's hands flew to her ears. A few weeks earlier, the deaconess had boxed them because Sarah had whispered to John. "It's no fun having your ears boxed," she admitted.

John made an awful face. "It's worse being whipped with a birch rod. All I did was smile when Elder Brewster told about poor old Jonah sitting in the hot sun and grumbling because a worm had eaten the plant that had given him shade."

John stretched and yawned. "It just seems like Jonah would have learned his lesson after the big fish spit him out and he was safe."

"It just seems like you would learn *your* lesson after you got us in trouble," Sarah teased.

He only grinned. "Run back to bed, little sister. It's almost time for Father and Mother to get up."

"I may be a whole lot shorter, but I'm only two years younger than you are," Sarah reminded him. "And say what you will, life in Leiden is never going to be the same." She scooted out the door and tiptoed to her own room, and a few minutes later John heard her clatter to breakfast in the wooden shoes she liked so well.

As the day continued, John had to admit that Sarah was right about life in Leiden changing. Gossip and rumors ran wild in every home, in factories, and in fields. His neighbor Hans, who was six months older than John, was full of news about war.

"It's feared that Spain will attack Holland," the tall, blond boy told John as they walked along the canal. "If Spain wins, Holland will become a Catholic country instead of a Protestant one, and Spain's royal family will rule over us. I only wish I were older and could sign up on a Dutch ship. Then I'd be able to protect my country."

"Some of the older boys from our group already have," John said. "What an adventure that would be."

"Almost as much of an adventure as that wild tale I've heard about some of your people going to the New World," Hans said, his long legs easily keeping pace with John. "Do you know anything about it?"

"There's been a lot of talk," John answered, careful not to reveal what his parents had told him, "but no one's made any final decision that I've heard of. Of course, people are worried that we wouldn't be able to worship freely if Holland lost the war."

"No need to worry about that," Hans argued. "We've got a navy that's more than ready to defend us. Besides," he added, his blue eyes lighting up with mischief, "if you left Leiden, who'd be able to challenge me in those skating races every winter?"

"Good point," John agreed, "although this winter *you'd* better be ready to be the challenger. I'm planning on winning those races." He glanced regretfully up at the sun. "It's getting late. I'd better run home and get my chores done."

"That's the problem with you English," Hans teased. "You don't know how to have fun."

John simply waved in reply as he dashed toward home, but his thoughts were troubled. Eager as he was for his family to leave for America, he would miss his fun-loving friends in Holland. *And for all I know, we may not leave at all,* he admitted to himself. All he could do was wait and pray that God would let Father and the others know the best thing to do. A decision must and would be made soon.

Maybe even tomorrow.

CHAPTER 3

A Startling Announcement

Two days later, John Smythe ran down the cobblestoned street toward home as fast as his long legs could carry him. Head back, elbows bent, arms swinging, he panted from running so hard but refused to slow his pace.

John's heart pounded. Only this morning he had by chance heard of a secret meeting between Elder William Brewster and other leaders of their group. Elder Brewster was in hiding because he and Edward Winslow had smuggled pamphlets to Scotland and England condemning the king! King James had ordered their arrest, but so far the Dutch government had not been able to find them.

When John raced past the University of Leiden, he nearly ran into his pastor, John Robinson. Even though he was a pastor, John Robinson also studied and taught at the university.

"What's the hurry?" Robinson laughed, dropping a friendly arm around the boy's shoulder.

"I have to get home," John said, breathing heavily. He usually enjoyed talking with his minister, but not today. News burned on his tongue, but Father and Mother frowned on talebearing. Unless something was absolutely true, their children were not to repeat it. Even if it was true, they were to discuss it only within their own family. That way no one would be hurt by idle gossip.

"Then Godspeed, lad." John Robinson lifted his arm, and the lanky boy shot off faster than an arrow from a strong bow.

When he reached his home, John burst into the house. Taking precautions to keep his voice low, he called, "We are going! Father, Mother, Sarah, we are going to America!"

"Calm yourself, John," his mother quietly said. She patted a low stool next to the loom where she sat weaving. "Father isn't home from the factory yet, and I sent Sarah with food baskets for the poor." She sighed. "Our people are sick from working too hard, especially the children. They look like little old men and women. Perhaps it is selfish, but I cannot help thanking God that you and Sarah are spared the long hours so many must work to keep food on the table. It also allows us to help others in need."

"Things will be better in America," John promised. He half closed his eyes, dreaming of the New World. "There are no kings to say we cannot take game from the forest. There are no kings to tax us and persecute us. Mother, we will be free."

Not until that moment had John realized how much he desired freedom. He had thought only of the adventures they would surely have, the excitement of crossing an ocean and living in a new country.

Just then Sarah came in, carrying her now-empty baskets. "Sarah, we will be free," John repeated.

"What are you talking about?" Sarah asked.

"We are going to America to be free. I will tell you the rest when Father comes home."

Sarah stared silently at John. Her lips drooped, and her eyes looked enormous in her pale face.

"Sarah, dear, would you please bring me a cup of water?" Mother asked. As soon as Sarah left the room, Mother told John, "Deal gently with her, my son. She is young and also fearful, as am I."

"You aren't afraid, are you, Mother?" John's mouth fell open in astonishment. "Why, you came from England and—"

"I came because we had no choice if we were to remain true to our teachings and our God." Mother's hands lay idle in her aproned lap, and her green eyes so like Sarah's held shadows. "If we go to the New World, it will be for the same reason. Our group here is growing smaller and smaller."

John thought of the small cottages near Green Gate, their meetinghouse. The poorest of their group lived in them. The Smythes were a little better off. They lived near a few other members on a narrow street. John had once shocked Sarah by declaring, "I am glad we don't live in *Stincksteeg*, as the Brewsters do. Imagine, having a home in a place that means 'Smelly Alley'!"

Now he soberly asked, "Is Father ever afraid?" It seemed impossible for tall, strong William Smythe to be afraid of anything.

"Many times." Mother smiled. "He is also one of the bravest men I know."

"How can he be brave and frightened at the same time?" John demanded.

27

Sarah spoke from the doorway, her hand holding a cup of water for Mother. "He's brave because he goes ahead and does what he must, even though he's afraid. That's really being brave, isn't it, Mother? A lot braver than if a person isn't frightened."

"I never thought of that, but you're right." John leaped up from the stool. He thought of what his mother had asked him to do and added, "Sarah, you're a lot braver than you think you are."

His sister blushed with pleasure. "Thank you." A cheerful whistle came from outside the door. "Father's home. Now you can tell us what you know, John."

The moment William Smythe set foot inside the door, John spoke. "Our leaders had a meeting last night," he announced, feeling important to be the bearer of such news, but speaking in a quiet voice that would not carry beyond the walls and into the street. "It is as you said, Father. We cannot go back to England. Most of our friends there have been put in prison. Our leaders speak of a colony in the New World called Virginia. They say we can also go there and start a colony, one where we can live and worship as we choose."

"How do you know these things?" his father wanted to know. "I hope you have not been guilty of spying again."

John felt his face warm at the word *again,* but he proudly said, "No, sir. I overheard John Carver talking with some men on the street, but I wasn't spying. I didn't act like I heard him, for fear he'd be upset." He took a deep breath and dropped his voice to a whisper. "The best news is that some

English merchants may lend us money for the trip!"

"Are you speaking truth or jest, son?" Father sharply asked.

"Truth," John boldly stated. "John Carver said that if we agree to repay the English merchants with fish and furs and lumber from the New World, the merchants will lend us money to hire a ship, a crew, and supplies enough to take us to America."

"What about King James?" Sarah looked frightened. "He will never let us go."

"John Carver said the king will be more than happy to give permission. That way we will be farther away from him than ever, and he won't be troubled by us!"

Father laughed, and Mother joined in. Even Sarah smiled a bit.

"What will we do, Father?" John asked. "Will our family go to America?"

Father and Mother exchanged a look, and Sarah's face grew even more pale.

"We will listen to the advice of our leaders and pray for God's wisdom. Then your mother and I will decide," Father said firmly. "You and Sarah can help by praying for all of our families as we make this decision."

The news John had overheard soon ran through Leiden. John Carver and the other leaders urged their followers to leave. Yet when the final vote was taken, less than half wanted to leave Holland immediately. John and Sarah's parents were among those who had decided to leave. To their great disappointment, Pastor John Robinson quietly said he would stay behind.

"I will come later," he promised those who planned to sail. "For now, I must remain with the part of my flock who are not going to America at this time." Sadness over the coming separation lined his kind face. "Pray that it will not be long."

As they left the meeting, Sarah was very quiet. John dropped back next to her and whispered, "What's wrong?"

She looked up at him, and a tear slid down her freckled cheek. "I'm just thinking of all the friends we'll have to leave behind. There's good Pastor Robinson and the families who are staying here. Then there are my Dutch friends like Gretchen. No one our age is leaving for America."

"Would you rather we stayed behind and watched Mother and Father leave on the ship?" John asked. "Our friends who are staying won't see their parents for at least a year, probably longer."

"No," Sarah admitted. She sighed. "Leaving people you love is hard to do."

"Yes, it is," agreed Mother, turning to join their conversation. "But we won't be leaving for weeks, maybe even months. There are many arrangements to make. Why, we don't even have a ship to sail on yet. You and I will be extra busy packing things for our trip, Sarah, but you can invite Gretchen to visit us while we work as often as her parents will allow."

For the first time since they'd left the meeting, a faint smile crossed Sarah's face.

As the weeks passed, John realized the truth of Mother's words. Nothing was happening, or so it seemed. Dutch and English companies offered to finance the trip, but only if the travelers worked for them like slaves. The only good thing that happened took place in England. When King James heard about the proposed trip and that the group expected to support itself by fishing, he supposedly said, "So God have my soul! 'Tis an honest trade! It was the apostles' own calling."

"Good news," Father finally announced one evening as he arrived home from work. "A man named John Weston says that seventy men called 'Adventurers' are ready and waiting to supply money for the ships, crew, and supplies. Of course, there are certain conditions."

"Is the offer any better than the earlier ones?" Mother asked.

For once, John was able to bite his tongue and stand quietly to one side. He wanted to hear what his father had to say, and he knew that if he interrupted he might be sent out of the room.

"We'll work for the investors for seven years," Father said. "That's not good, but it's the best offer we've had, and our leaders don't think we'll get one that's better." Father sighed. "We not only need money to charter a ship to take us from England to America, with crew and supplies enough for many weeks, but we must also purchase a ship to carry us from

Holland to Southampton. Both ships will cross the Atlantic once we meet in England."

The Adventurers' offer created a lot of debate among those who would be traveling. John sometimes felt like he would burst with impatience. Why must everything take so long? Why couldn't people see how important it was to leave Holland? He listened to the ringing words of William Bradford.

"Great difficulties always go with great and honorable actions. They must be faced with courage. Granted, the dangers are great. They are not desperate. The difficulties will be many, but some of the things we fear may never come to pass! Others can be prevented by using wisdom. Through the help of God and patience, we can bear them or overcome them.

"We should neither make attempts that are rash nor undertake things lightly or out of curiosity and hope for gain. Our reasons are good and honorable. We have every right to expect the blessing of God."

John squirmed uncomfortably when William Bradford spoke of curiosity, but his heart raced. Would he one day be a man like this? Or would he be like Father—quieter, but equally determined to take his family to a place that offered freedom and the chance to prosper?

A secret prayer slipped from John's heart. *Make me strong. There will be much to do. I know You will go with us to America.* He longed with all his excited young heart to add *And please, make it soon* but decided against it. God might not think it polite for a twelve-year-old boy to tell Him to hurry.

In spite of John's unfinished prayer, the "soon" he longed

for came before he expected it. The very next day, exciting news reached Leiden. A sixty-ton ship named the *Speedwell* had been bought and was already on her way!

CHAPTER 4

Only the Brave

"The *Speedwell* will carry us to England," John told Sarah for at least the fiftieth time. "Even now the *Mayflower* is being loaded with supplies and getting ready to meet us at Southampton. Just think. Soon we will be on our way." He searched her face for the excitement that flamed higher and higher inside him.

Sarah didn't answer. Neither did she catch fire from his promise. "If only things had been better here." She looked at her brother curiously. "Aren't you going to miss Holland at all? What about your friend Hans? And aren't you even a little bit afraid?"

"Of course." John remembered Mother's words about dealing gently with Sarah. "It's really scary knowing we're going so far away. I'll miss my races with Hans. I'll miss the young men who have married Dutch girls and won't be going with us, and those who are too old or sick to sail. It will be hard to be separated for even a little while from friends who are our own age."

He patted Sarah's hand. "After we get to the New World and build a colony, others will come. You'll see."

"I suppose," Sarah grumbled. "But I'd much rather stay here." Her face brightened. "At least this afternoon I'll be able to work with Gretchen."

Shortly after the noon meal, a knock sounded at the door, and Sarah opened it to greet her friend. As energetic as she was tiny, Gretchen's bubbly personality filled the kitchen where she joined Sarah and Mother in their work.

Sarah looked enviously at Gretchen's bright blue dress. Unlike Sarah's people, Dutch children dressed in beautiful colors, and Sarah sometimes wondered what it would be like to wear something other than drab browns and blacks.

"It must be so exciting for you," Gretchen enthused as she salted pork and got it ready for drying. "I wish my family would do something so adventurous."

"You should get together with my brother, John," Sarah said. "All he can talk about are the adventures we're going to have. But what about the dangers?"

"That's true," Gretchen admitted. "I've heard stories about sickness and storms at sea that would curl your hair."

"Girls, girls," Mother interrupted. "Let's not get carried away by wild tales. We have work to do."

The two friends turned back to their tasks, but Sarah grew sad as she thought of leaving her friend.

"I wish you could come with us," she whispered to Gretchen.

"I do, too," Gretchen confided. "But we have lots of time to spend together before you leave, and I'm planning a surprise for you before you go."

"Surprise? What surprise?" Sarah asked.

"You'll find out when it's time," Gretchen teased and then went to the pump to wash her hands before she left for home.

Just after Gretchen had left, John rushed home with a book, its cover worn from being passed hand to hand.

"Look at this book!" he shouted.

"You do not need to shout for us to hear you," his mother gently reproved. "Now what is your latest treasure, and where did you get it?"

"It's a copy of Captain John Smith's report on the New World, *A Description of New England*," John answered eagerly, but in a softer tone. "I met John Carver in the street, and he asked me to bring it home. Everyone who's going to the New World is getting a chance to read it, so we'll know what to expect."

That evening after dinner, the Smythe family eagerly studied Captain Smith's glowing descriptions of the New World. Captain Smith was not only a former governor of the colony of Jamestown, Virginia, but he was also an explorer. He had sailed the New England coast and mapped its harbors.

"America is wonderful," the captain promised. "A land where those willing to work can prosper. I urge people to leave their homes across the water and settle in this untouched, unspoiled country."

As they read each page, Father and John grew more enthusiastic about their trip. "You've heard what the explorers and fishermen say," Father added at one point. "They describe great forests filled with nut and fruit trees, deer, and wild boar. The soil is fertile, and they say there are so many fish along the coast, a man can drop a net and come up with a great haul! Some even say a fortune could be made from the fur trade."

Mother said little, but the next day, she and Sarah spent even more time sorting and packing. Sarah at last accepted that they were leaving and began saying good-bye to the land of her birth, spending every spare moment with Gretchen.

Days later, word came of a great tragedy. Father came home with the sad news. "One hundred and thirty of our countrymen have perished making the crossing," he told his family. "The Atlantic Ocean is dangerous, but it is not the sea that took them. They died from hunger, sickness, and lack of water."

He dropped his head into his hands. "Sometimes I wonder if our brothers and sisters who choose to remain in Holland are right."

John sprang to his feet. His eyes flashed. "No, Father!" His young voice rang in the quiet room. Mother shot him a warning look, and he quickly returned to his chair.

"Father, I apologize for speaking to you so abruptly," John quickly said.

"Your apology is accepted," Father said, lifting his head and looking at his son. "But I think you have something to say. Tell me what is on your heart."

"I was just thinking," John said, "did not God open a way by causing the wealthy merchants to give us money for the trip? Did not our own John Carver and Robert Cushman go to King James himself and get a grant of land in the New World?"

"The king did not issue approval," Father reminded him. "He only said he would not stand in our way or trouble us if we conducted ourselves peacefully."

Speaking earnestly, John leaned forward. "It is not as though we were going to America to grow rich, although our leaders say we are bound to be better off there than we are here. We are going because we need a place where we can worship God and read the Bible for ourselves. What if Moses had let tales of the wilderness fill his heart with fear? What if he had not followed God's leading but had told his people to stay in Egypt and obey the pharaoh?"

John saw his father's shoulders straighten and some of the old fire come back to his troubled face.

"You are right, son," Father said. "Elder Bradford says when we sail from Holland, we will become pilgrims, people who go on a long, long journey. We are pilgrims for the Lord, not for what we think we might gain." He took a deep breath. "Even Jesus became a pilgrim when He left His home and traveled to those who needed to hear His message."

A new thought struck John. "Jesus died for everyone. The Indians in America have a right to hear about Him, don't they? How can they hear if Christians don't go tell them?"

"Gretchen says the Indians are savages." Sarah's eyes rounded with fear. "She told me they steal children. She says we will have to go naked and be hungry and maybe get scalped."

"How does she know?" John demanded. "She hasn't been to America, has she? Do you think Gretchen is wiser than our leaders?"

"Children, children." Mother held up a hand. "Remember our family rule. Each may speak freely, but we do not argue.

Besides, both of you are right! We cannot help but fear the unknown, yet the same God who saw us safely to Holland can and will go with us to America."

"Why did He not save the people who died crossing the ocean?" Sarah asked.

"Come here, child." Father held out both arms, and Sarah ran to him. He held her close and said, "We cannot always know why God does or does not do things the way we think He should. We can only trust Him. Sarah, you know that even if something should happen, we have Jesus' promise that we will go where He is and live with Him. Can we ask for more?"

She shook her head and wiped away tears with the back of her hand.

"There. Now run along and help your mother with the packing. John is right. We cannot turn back." His brown eyes so like his son's twinkled. "Abigail, I fancy this son of ours may one day become a preacher! He has certainly given us something to consider this day."

John couldn't help grinning, even though he knew his face, neck, and ears must be bright red. "I only spoke what I believe to be true."

Father slowly said, "That is what God expects us to do." He gave John a warning look. "We also need to remember one thing: Sometimes our beliefs may be wrong. It is important to study the Bible and pray. That way we can separate man's ways from God's."

"Yes, sir." John liked it when Father spoke to him man to man. He carefully tucked the bit of advice away for a future time when he would need it.

Preparations for the voyage went steadily forward, although the number of people who agreed to sail continued to drop. It took time for the Smythes and their friends to gather what they needed to take with them. When John's father got home from work, he and John carefully collected the outdoor equipment they'd need for building their new home, hunting, and growing food.

"If I were around next winter," John told his friend Hans one afternoon, "I'd be sure to skate faster than you on the frozen canals. Look at how much bigger my muscles have gotten from carrying and packing all these things."

"That's impressive," Hans agreed. "What are you taking?"

"Well, so far we've crated up axes and saws as well as lanterns and shovels. Then there are the nails, spades, and chisels, as well as the hammers."

"It's hard to imagine living in a place where you can't simply buy food and cloth and other things you need," Hans said.

"It's even harder actually packing all those things that we'll need," John said, ruefully rubbing a sore arm.

That evening when John and Father began packing again, Hans came over. "My parents said I could help you pack if you could use the help," he offered.

"Gratefully accepted," Father said, shaking Hans's hand. "Tonight we're tackling more of our tools—vises, pitchforks, and planes—and if we have time, we'll start packing some cart wheels."

"What else will you be taking?" Hans asked.

"Well, we'll need the cart, plough, and wheelbarrow for farming and transporting things. Our larger group is taking some canoes for exploring the rivers and streams. And the women and girls are busy getting all the pots, dishes, medicines, and clothing—to say nothing of looms and food—together. Sarah and her mother have been working for weeks to make sure we have enough food and clothing to survive. They've even packed a spit for cooking over a fire and a mortar for grinding grain."

"Won't the ship be providing food for the journey?" Hans asked.

"Yes, but because we're leaving in the summer, we'll need enough food for a year once we get to Virginia. We won't be able to plant seed until the spring or harvest crops until next fall."

"Let's hope you have a good harvest," Hans said.

"God will provide," Father answered, and they went to work.

After a couple hours of hard work, Father and the boys decided it was time to go in the house and have something to eat and drink. They found Sarah and Mother going over a stack of labeled provisions.

"I think we're ready for some rest, too," Mother greeted them.

"How is the work progressing?" Father asked.

"Well, we have most of the dried goods taken care of. There are thirty-two bushels of meal and eight bushels each of dried peas and oatmeal for the four of us."

Hans's eyes widened.

"Fresh fruit won't last long," Mother continued to explain, "so we're packing dried prunes, raisins, and currants. We should be able to get sugar and molasses in the New World from the West Indies, but we're packing as many spices as we can afford."

"I never thought of how much food one family could eat in a year," Hans said, unable to restrain himself.

"And that doesn't include the oil and vinegar we'll take to season and preserve food," Sarah added.

"Are you taking any lemon juice?" Hans asked. "I've heard that's the only thing they know of that can keep you from getting scurvy."

"You're right," Mother said.

"You mean we'll have to drink that sour stuff?" John protested, his face twisting up at the thought.

"Better to drink a little sour lemon juice than to have bleeding gums and become very sick," Father replied.

"I suppose," John said, "but I can't say I'm excited about the thought."

"That's probably the only thing about this trip you aren't excited about," teased Hans. "Thank you for the food, Mistress Smythe. It's getting late, so I'd better run home now."

"Thank you for your help," Father said.

After the family had said good-bye to Hans and were preparing for evening prayers, John thought about the upcoming voyage.

"We will have a good time on board ship," he said to Sarah. "Even if our friends won't be going, there will be older children on board. Love and Wrasling Brewster are going, although their parents are leaving the rest of their children behind. Bartholomew, Remember, and Mary Collins are also going. So is

Resolved White and ever so many more—"

He broke off. "Sarah, more than half of the forty-one people who will sail from Leiden are children! Isn't that exciting?"

"Yes, it is," Sarah cautiously agreed. "You didn't say anything about Elder Bradford's son John. Isn't he going?"

"I don't know," John admitted, although he hated to confess that there was anything about the voyage that he didn't know. Sometimes Sarah teased him and called him the town crier, after the officers who went through English villages crying out the news to the people.

"Only in your case," she had said, "you carry the news to our family."

Each day brought the Smythes and their friends closer to departure. Each day saw those who refused to leave Holland sharpen their criticism of those who would sail.

One day, John was returning from the wharf when he came upon a group of people surrounding William Bradford. Curious about what was happening, John quietly stood on the edge of the group and listened.

"Why?" tearful members pleaded. "Do you think God wants loved ones separated for years, perhaps forever? Give up this mad scheme. You are weak in the faith to feel you must run away. War with the Spaniards may never come. Even if it does, God can care for His people. If you trust Him as He commands, why do you cross an ocean that may swallow you alive?"

"Oh ye of little faith," William Bradford thundered. "Will you cling to homes where your children daily grow more like the Dutch? Even now they rebel at having to attend meeting.

Look at those around you. Women wearing breeches. Families laughing and dancing on the Sabbath."

He sternly looked around the circle of faces. "You quote Scripture to fit your purposes and forget the commandment given by the apostle Paul: 'Wherefore come out from among them, and be ye separate, saith the Lord, and touch not the unclean thing; and I will receive you.'"

Bradford proudly flung his head up. "I turned my back on my family. I left England, the country I love. God gave me strength to do so, and He has kept the promise given in the next verse: 'And [I] will be a Father unto you, and ye shall be my sons and daughters, saith the Lord Almighty.' Let the babble of those who follow the dictates of their conscience and remain in Holland cease. We also follow our conscience, and our Master."

The ringing words sank deep in John Smythe's heart. He shouted "Amen!" along with other supporters who stood nearby. John knew if he lived to be a white-haired, bent old man, he would never forget this moment when only the brave chose to sail.

CHAPTER 5

The *Speedwell* Doesn't

"I am so glad they scrubbed down both ships," Sarah Smythe confessed to her brother, John. She made a horrible face. "I can't bear to think of the bugs and rats on ships!"

John heaved a bushel of oatmeal to one side of the great store of provisions, proud of being strong and able to do hard work. The New World needed men, not weak boys. "The *Speedwell* is being completely overhauled."

He stopped and panted, wiping away the sweat from his face. The July day was warm and sunny. "She's being repaired, too, and given taller masts and larger sails. Otherwise she could never keep up with the *Mayflower*. She should be ready to sail by the last day of this month." He felt a pang of jealousy. "I wish we were going on the *Mayflower*, like the London Strangers. She's three times bigger than the *Speedwell* and weighs one hundred eighty tons!"

He wrinkled his nose. "She smells better, too. The *Mayflower* is called a 'sweet ship,' because she doesn't have bad smells like ships that carry fish."

"Well, we can't go on the *Mayflower*," Sarah told him. "We could barely afford to buy the *Speedwell*, even with the money the English merchants lent us. It's big enough to hold what few of us are going and most of the provisions. Don't forget, the ship and crew are going to stay a year with us in America."

"You're right." John grinned at her. "The *Mayflower* will stay just long enough for us to load it with cargo then sail back to England. The London emigrants are only renting it."

"Why do we call them Strangers?"

John couldn't help tormenting his sister. "You're getting as curious as I am, always asking why."

She smirked and repeated what he always told her. "How can I learn anything if I don't ask questions?"

John joined in her laughter, glad to see the gloom of the last weeks lifting from her freckled face, at least for a time. "Remember what Father said? The London emigrants aren't going to the New World for religious reasons, but to see if they can find a better life. It's a good thing they are traveling with us, though. If there's trouble, they'll be there to help us. We'll do the same for them. We'll stay in sight of each other all the time, just in case."

"What kind of trouble?" Sarah looked suspicious.

John thought as quickly as he could. "Uh, you know. Like if there's a bad storm."

Or pirate ships that rove the sea, attack cargo ships, and seize their goods, a little voice inside whispered. John wasn't about to tell Sarah that! She was still frightened enough of the wild Atlantic Ocean they must cross, with its white-foam waves and mighty swells. The longer she went without hearing about pirates, the better. Anyway, they might not see a pirate the whole time they were sailing.

Five days. Four. Three. Two. The day before departure from Leiden arrived at last. Pastor John Robinson ordered a time of fasting and prayer. A solemn group gathered for the last time.

John tore his attention from the future long enough to realize how final this day was in the lives of everyone present. Unexpected pain poked red-hot needles into him. Why couldn't they just go without saying any good-byes?

He looked around the room. One day he would again see some of those remaining in Holland, for they had promised to come on another crossing. Others, especially the old and sick members of his congregation, he would not meet again until they all reached heaven where there were no sad farewells.

A wave of love threatened to undo his courage and eagerness to sail. So did some of the prayers and Pastor Robinson's farewell sermon.

John scrubbed at his stinging eyes and felt relieved when the meeting ended. In a short while, he and his family would take the first steps of the long journey that lay ahead.

"God, go with us," John whispered. He turned to Sarah, at last knowing how she felt. Tears streamed from her green eyes. Her chin wobbled, but she held her head high. John had never been prouder of his younger sister. Already Leiden seemed part of the past.

That afternoon, John and Hans took one last walk together along the canal. They were unusually quiet. Jokes seemed out of place, and they were uncomfortable admitting what they felt.

Finally, as they turned up their street, Hans stopped and

looked at John. "I'll miss you, John," he said, his eyes suspiciously moist. "I've never had a friend like you, and I don't know that I ever will again. I don't really understand why your family must leave, but I respect you for doing what you believe is right."

"I'll miss you, too, Hans," John said. "And I'll never forget you as long as I live. But don't forget when you win all those canal races that the only reason you're winning is because I'm not here to challenge you."

Awkwardly the boys smiled at each other. Hans held out his hand, and he and John exchanged a strong handshake before turning into their separate homes.

John paused in the dark hallway to rub his eyes and wait for his heart to stop pounding. He didn't want Sarah to know how hard it was for him to leave his friends. As he stood by the door, he heard sniffling coming from the parlor.

Curious, he peered around the partly opened parlor door and saw Sarah sitting in a corner, quietly crying into a handkerchief.

"What's wrong, Sarah?" John asked, rushing over to her.

"I. . .just said. . .good-bye. . .to Gretchen," she sobbed. "She gave me this as a surprise. . .so I wouldn't for. . .forget her." Sarah held out the damp handkerchief that Gretchen had embroidered with a tulip and their names.

"I know how you feel," John said, sitting down beside his sister and putting an arm across her shoulders.

"You do?" she asked, amazement crossing her freckled face. "But I thought you were all excited about leaving tomorrow."

"I am," John admitted. "But I just said good-bye to Hans,

and I don't think I've ever had to do anything more difficult in my life."

John and Sarah sat together in companionable silence for a few minutes until they were ready to finish up the last jobs that needed to be done before their trip. John had never felt quite so close to his sister.

The next day dawned with good weather, but none of the forty-one people who were about to leave Leiden noticed. Slowly, they filed onto canal boats that would take them about twenty-four miles to Delftshaven. Friends, family members, and Pastor Robinson accompanied them. If some felt like cheering, they hid it well. Most faces were even more sober than usual.

The Smythes were one of the few families not leaving brothers and sisters, a grandfather, or grandmother behind, but the pain of the coming separation hung around them like a heavy, gray blanket.

"Come." Father took Mother's arm and helped her into a canal boat.

John roused from his thoughts, nimbly hopped in, and held out a hand to Sarah. She turned her head to glance behind her. "Don't look back, Sarah. It will make it harder. Remember Leiden and our friends the way they were."

Surprise showed in her face. "All right." Sarah stared straight ahead. So did John, Mother, and Father. Within a few minutes, John put aside the past in favor of the present. The canal boats were nothing compared with the *Speedwell* or the

Mayflower. Eight hours later, they reached Delftshaven, a main shipping port in Holland.

"There she is!" John's shrill cry cut through the numbness of misery surrounding everyone. They stared at the *Speedwell,* ready and waiting by the East India House. From that dock, the Pilgrims would embark the next day on their great adventure. Impressive stone, brick, and iron buildings lined both sides of the canal.

Seeing the *Speedwell* did what nothing else had been able to accomplish. Spirits soared. Hope burned brightly once more. The group stayed in a building near the Old Church on the canal their last night in Holland. They ate, drank, laughed, and filled the air with songs of praise and thanksgiving. Even Sarah perked up.

"It isn't bad so far," she admitted to her brother.

"Not bad! It's better than I expected." He hastily added, "I'm glad you're feeling better."

"So am I." Sarah yawned. "I'm tired, though."

"We all are," Mother said and shooed them off to their sleeping pallets.

The next day arrived heavy with river mist. While leaving Leiden had been hard, the final good-byes at Voorhaven Quay were even worse. Great crowds of people had come to see the Pilgrims off. Friends from Amsterdam. The curious. Families. John wished they had all stayed in Leiden!

Sarah pinched his arm. She pointed to weeping Dorothy

Bradford. John swallowed hard. Dorothy clung to her little son, John, as if unable to tear herself away. He was to be left in the care of another family so she could go with her husband, William, on the *Speedwell*.

"How can she do it?" Sarah asked.

John didn't answer. He hadn't dreamed leaving would be this hard. Or that mothers would leave their children behind. What of Mistress Collins and Susanna White, both expecting additions to their families? He knew Susanna was taking a cradle for the baby who would be born in the New World. What if a baby came at sea? John squirmed and blushed. That was for the women to consider, not boys.

Mary Brewster stood close to her two daughters and son who would stay in Holland. Her husband, William, remained in hiding, still wanted by the police for printing illegal literature. Where was he?

Pastor Robinson led his flock in a final prayer. The emigrants hastily embraced loved ones a last time and boarded the *Speedwell*. Muskets fired. The ship's cannons boomed. People waved from deck and land. White sails billowed. The *Speedwell*, clearly identified as Dutch by the colorful flag on her mast, began to move. The ship followed the wide Maas River into the North Sea. Down the Strait of Dover. Into the English Channel that Mother and Father had mentioned in their stories of leaving England before John and Sarah were born.

None of the Smythes looked back. They fixed their gaze straight ahead and trusted God. Surely He would see them through whatever hardships or heartache they might face in order to worship Him in a free country.

Living space on the *Speedwell* proved to be far worse than expected. Even though the ship had been cleaned, the lower decks were horrible. People crowded together in damp rooms with little air and less light. Cooking could only be done when the sea stayed calm, for fear that sparks in the fire boxes might be carried by the wind and start a fire on the ship. Buckets served as toilets.

One day Sarah and John stood by the ship's rail, faces turned westward. "Can we live this way all across the Atlantic Ocean?" Sarah asked John in a troubled voice. "Why aren't things any better?"

John shrugged. "The more room passengers take, the less cargo the ship will hold. I wonder if Father would let me sleep on deck with the sailors."

"You know he wouldn't!" Sarah turned pale. "I heard John Carver say the sailors hate us. I don't know why. You might not be safe on deck."

John reluctantly gave up the idea. Sometimes the smell of so many people crowded together in such a small space made him feel sick. It would be so much better to sleep topside where at least the air was fresh. "Sarah, do you want to hear a riddle?"

"Is it funny?"

"Yes."

"Tell me quickly, please. There hasn't been a lot to laugh about since we left Delftshaven."

Her quick reply showed John how miserable she was. He felt sorry for her. Boys were allowed more freedom on the ship than girls. It couldn't be much fun for Sarah. She didn't like to poke into things and explore as he did, for fear of being caught and getting into trouble.

"Cheer up," he told her. "The voyage won't last forever."

"I hope not! What's the riddle?"

"The *Speedwell* doesn't."

"Doesn't what?" Sarah stared at him blankly.

"Doesn't *speed well.*" He chuckled. "Understand? The ship doesn't speed well. It lumbers along like a sick cow!"

Sarah rolled her eyes at her brother's poor attempt at humor. "It's not that slow. We'll be in Southampton tomorrow, and it's only been a few days." She turned toward John. A strong breeze filled the sails and ruffled her brown braids.

"I know, and then we will really, truly get started on our journey."

"Hey, you two, get away from that rail!" someone shouted.

John and Sarah whirled around. An angry-looking sailor came charging down the deck straight toward them!

CHAPTER 6

"I'll Feed You to the Fishes!"

The angry sailor came straight at John and Sarah, running down the deck at top speed. "Get away from that rail!" he bellowed again. He added a string of foreign words that sounded like they might be curses.

Sarah clapped her hands over her ears and stepped back from the charging man.

Not John. He stepped in front of Sarah and planted himself with feet apart and hands on his hips. His eyes darkened from clear brown to storm cloud black. "We aren't doing anything wrong."

"I'll teach you to talk back to me, you disrespectful whelp!" The sailor raised his brawny arm. He shook a hamlike fist and lunged closer, so close a blast of fishy breath came from between his cracked lips.

Sarah froze, unable to tear her gaze from the ugly, threatening face. She couldn't move an inch, even if her life depended on it. From the looks of the sailor, it just might!

John reached a long arm back and gave her a push. "Run!"

His order freed her feet. Sobbing, Sarah gathered her long skirts and obeyed. She kept her head turned so she could see John. Not heeding where she was going, the terrified girl crashed into something tall and solid. She let out a shriek and struggled against the strong hands that kept her from falling. "Let me go!"

"Sarah, child, what is it?"

Sarah looked up into the kindly face of Dr. Samuel Fuller, physician and surgeon, who traveled alone to the New World. She sagged against him. "The sailor!" she gasped. "He's going to kill John!"

"I doubt that." The good doctor sounded amused.

Sarah twisted in Dr. Fuller's arms and looked back. She heard the sailor roar, "I'm gonna feed you to the fishes!" Several other grinning sailors had stopped their work to see the fun, yelling catcalls to the man facing John. Fear for her brother overcame Sarah's terror. She tried to break free from Dr. Fuller's arms. "I have to help John," she cried. "Let me go!"

"He doesn't need any help," Dr. Fuller chuckled. "The lout has to catch John before he can hurt him. I don't think he can. If he does, I will interfere."

Only partly reassured, Sarah stopped struggling and watched. The bulky seaman was indeed no match for John's nimble feet. The boy danced away from danger on legs made strong from running through the streets of Leiden and skating the frozen canals. He led the bellowing sailor a merry chase, up and down the deck, around great stacks of cargo. The lumbering man simply could not catch the boy who ran like lightning.

A new voice shouted above the noise, "Klaus, what is the meaning of this?" The captain of the *Speedwell* stepped directly into the charging sailor's path and glared at him.

The seaman stumbled to a halt. "Just havin' a bit o' fun wi' the lad." He touched his hand to his cap in a rough salute, but his face turned clammy white.

Sarah's eyes opened wide with astonishment. "Why—"

Dr. Fuller placed his hand gently over her mouth. "Keep silent, child. No need to make things worse than they already are."

The captain looked suspiciously from his laughing crew to John, who had halted a short distance away and stood leaning against the rail. "Is that all it is? Answer me, boy!" His voice cut the tense air like a whip.

John hesitated. Sarah saw him look at the sailor who had lied then shrug his shoulders, a movement his sister knew could be taken as either yes or no.

"All right, then. Keep away from my sailors, you hear?"

"Yes, sir." A lock of brown hair dangled over John's forehead. He grinned and said, "That's what I was trying to do," in his most innocent voice.

"Haw haw!" All of the sailors except the one who had started the trouble burst out laughing. Klaus gave John a strange look. It still held anger, but a gleam of respect also shone in his eyes.

"Get back to work, all of you!" the captain barked.

"Aye, aye." The group broke up, still laughing.

John turned toward Sarah. His eyes sparkled with excitement and looked like twin stars, until he saw the doctor. Then his jaw dropped and he cast a quick glance around them. "What. . .did you. . .I didn't know you were here," he stuttered.

"I suspected as much." Dr. Fuller folded his arms over his stomach. "John, John, what are we going to do with you?"

All John's boldness vanished, and he hung his head.

Sarah slipped a comforting hand in the crook of his elbow. "It wasn't his fault," she loyally defended. "All we did was stand by the rail. The sailor started yelling at us, and John told him we weren't doing anything wrong."

"Wouldn't it have been better to hold your tongue?" Dr. Fuller asked.

"Beggin' yer pardon, sir, but that's just what the lad did," a low voice said.

The doctor and the two children turned. John's pursuer stood just behind them, breathing heavily. Sarah felt the blood drain from her face. He must have sneaked back as soon as the captain left the deck. *What will happen now?* She could see the same question in John's and Dr. Fuller's eyes when she looked at them.

"The matter is settled," the doctor exclaimed. "Go about your work."

Klaus didn't budge. "Not afore I thank the lad," he stubbornly said. His hand shot out and swallowed John's. "He saved me from the cat-o'-nine-tails by holdin' his tongue." He gripped John's hand with his huge paw, and what passed for a smile twitched across his lips.

John's mouth dropped open. Sarah gulped. Dr. Fuller chuckled again. The sailor's face dropped back into its usual ferocious look. "Keep away from that rail," he warned John. "You, too." He glared at Sarah, whose eyes grew wide. "Last voyage a brat fell in the brine durin' a storm. Who fished him out? Me. Klaus. Nearly drowned. Shoulda let the fishes get him. It woulda served him right fer hangin' on the rail." The rescuer scowled and trudged away, leaving the Smythes and the doctor speechless.

"Who would have thought it?" John marveled when the sailor got out of hearing. "Klaus, of all people, a hero! No wonder he yelled at us. I guess he was trying to scare us so much we'd never go near the ship's rail again, especially during a storm."

"You just never know who may be a real hero," Dr. Fuller told them. He cocked his head to one side. "I certainly don't recommend your method, John, but you may just have made yourself a friend." A shadow crept into his eyes. "Being whipped with a cat-o'-nine-tails is a terrible punishment. Some men die from the beatings."

Sarah thought of the cruel whip made of nine knotted cords fastened to a handle and used to keep crew members in line. She shivered. "No wonder Klaus was glad John didn't tell on him!"

John just looked thoughtful, but Dr. Fuller added, "Evidently somewhere beneath that crusty, bluffing, don't-care attitude lies a tender heart. Otherwise Klaus wouldn't have risked his own life by diving into a stormy ocean to save a child."

"It's hard to believe such a mean-looking person could do a good thing," protested Sarah.

"We cannot judge what is in a man's heart by what is on his face," Dr. Fuller said. "Remember what the Lord told Samuel about judging by what we see? He told Samuel, 'The Lord seeth not as man seeth; for man looketh on the outward appearance, but the Lord looketh on the heart.'"

John and Sarah kept their distance from the crew, just as the captain ordered. But every time they saw Klaus, they smiled at him.

Klaus either ignored them or grunted. He continued to scowl. He bellowed if he thought they were getting too close to the rail. Yet never again did Klaus double his fist and shake it at them. Neither did he challenge John to a footrace, as a few of the others did! Word sped through the ship that young John Smythe could outrun all of the boys and most of the men aboard.

When the *Speedwell* sailed into Southampton and dropped anchor next to the *Mayflower*, the larger ship loomed over her like a giant above a child. The *Mayflower* had come a week earlier with the sixty-one London Strangers who would sail on her to the New World. The two groups met at the West Quay, eager to meet their fellow travelers.

John and Sarah's parents and many other adults simply

stood and looked. Twelve long years had passed since they had stood on English soil. The emotion of the moment would stay with them a long time.

"Look at the holes in the fortress wall," John said.

Sarah was more interested in the comfortable cottages up and down the streets of Southampton. If only King James would allow her family freedom to worship in their own way, they could stay in England. How wonderful it would be to live right in one of the neat cottages in Southampton instead of being forced to sail thousands of miles to a new land.

"Come on, Sarah." John tugged at her hand. "Father says we may talk with the children." He pointed at a group running and calling to one another between the many crates and trunks piled on the dock.

"Are you sure it's all right?" She glanced at her parents and their friends, then back to the Strangers. What a difference! Sarah's people dressed plainly. The men wore tall, broad-brimmed hats, heavy clothing, warm stockings, and sturdy leather shoes. Women dressed in dark cloaks with hoods that tied under the chin over plain dresses with white collars and cuffs.

Not so the Strangers! Sarah gasped at the rainbow-bright colors, the feathers and trimmings and buttons and lace on their clothing. One young lady in particular dazzled Sarah. Sweet-faced and stylish, Priscilla Mullins smiled at the children from her place next to her shopkeeper father, William, her mother, and her brother, Joseph. Sarah felt glad they would be sailing on the *Mayflower*.

She also liked the large Hopkins family who came to greet her parents.

"I tried to get to America once before," Stephen Hopkins boomed. "The ship wrecked in the Bermudas. This time we'll have better luck. This is my wife, Elizabeth." The woman, obviously expecting a child, smiled at them. So did the Hopkins children: Giles, Constanta, and Damaris.

A young man named John Alden joined the group. Sarah liked his pleasant face and good manners. She laughed with the others when he confessed, "I've been working here in Southampton as a cooper, making tubs and casks. I've heard so much about this exciting voyage, I just signed up for a year with the company and will be sailing to America." John Alden glanced at pretty Priscilla Mullins, who blushed and looked down. Sarah thought it very romantic.

The one person neither Sarah nor John liked on first sight was a very short man named Myles Standish. He stood with his wife, Rose, and wore a sword to remind people he was a professional soldier and had fought many wars in Europe. He had flaming red hair and a face to match.

"He looks mean," John whispered.

"I know. I don't want to be around him," Sarah agreed.

"We don't have to worry until we reach the New World," John told her. "He'll be on the *Mayflower*, and we'll be on the *Speedwell*." The corners of his mouth turned down. "At least we will be if they ever get the leaks in our ship fixed."

A few hours later, more bad news reached the travelers. Thomas Weston, the man who had arranged financing, arrived with a new contract that included harsher rules. The group from Holland refused to sign it. Would this be the end of their dream?

CHAPTER 7

Discouraging Days

"How dare Thomas Weston bring such a contract?" John demanded of Father.

Father's eyes shot sparks the same way his son's often did when he was angry. "The sponsors have added two unbearable terms. They are ordering us to work for them seven days a week, but we must have two days to do our own work, or we cannot survive." He spread his hands wide. "The second demand is even worse. They want the homes we build to become company property!"

"Are they mad?" Mother cried. "We owned our homes even in Scrooby and Leiden. We'll be no better than slaves if our leaders agree to abide by the new rules!"

"We cannot and shall not agree to their demands," Father replied.

His prediction came true. The leaders flatly refused to even consider signing away the freedom they had struggled so hard to find and hoped to enjoy in the New World.

With his usual ability to be on the spot when anything important took place, John smuggled himself into the meeting with Thomas Weston where the amended contract was to be signed.

"We shall not labor seven days for the company. Our homes must be our own," the leaders stubbornly insisted.

Weston grew furious. He angrily reminded them of how hard he'd worked to get the money they needed for the voyage.

It did nothing to change the men's minds. At last Weston shouted, "You may look to stand on your own legs!" Although the businessmen remained financially responsible for the expedition, Weston got even with the Pilgrims for not signing the new contract. He refused to pay the port fees still owing on the *Mayflower* and left for London immediately.

"What shall we do?" the travelers asked. "If the bill is not paid, we will be in trouble with the authorities. King James may cancel our land grant in the New World and take back his permission for us to go."

John shuddered at the thought. They must go or be homeless.

"We don't have any money," someone pointed out. "How can we pay what we don't have?"

After much discussion, the people agreed to sell enough of the precious tubs of butter they had brought in their provisions to meet the debt. John slipped away from the meeting and told Sarah all about it. "We will have to go without butter because of Thomas Weston," he said glumly.

"I 'spect we'll have to go without a lot of things," Sarah said. Her freckled face looked solemn. "Father and Mother said Jesus probably didn't have butter when He was a pilgrim, either, so we shouldn't complain."

John felt ashamed. "They're right." He cheered up and

tweaked one of her braids. "The good news is, we're sailing as soon as the *Speedwell's* seams are recaulked. Hooray!" He turned a handspring.

At last they sailed. How the passengers celebrated! Not just because at long last they were on their way to America. Oh, no, they had another and far more wonderful reason.

William Brewster, still wanted as a prisoner by the English officials, was on the *Speedwell.*

Not even keen-eyed John Smythe knew how or when their favorite elder had come aboard. Somehow he had sneaked past the very persons looking for him and hidden himself. Once on the seas, he would be safe, at least for a time.

The celebration ended all too soon. Weather in the English Channel was so stormy, the *Speedwell* began to leak again. Pounding waves and high winds sent the ship reeling until the passengers wondered if she could ever right herself. The captain signaled the *Mayflower,* and the two ships sailed into Dartmouth, the nearest port, for repairs. Skilled carpenters spent ten days working on the *Speedwell* and said she was safe for the voyage.

During all this time, Elder Brewster was forced to remain in hiding. If he was discovered on English shores, he would be sent to a dungeon or maybe even hanged. Every man, woman, and child on board feared for his safety.

Not until early September could the expedition set out again. The weather was calm, and passengers prayed for more good weather. They passed Land's End, the last part of England they could see, and sailed on.

"This is more like it," John told Sarah, watching the sun set in a fiery splash on the ocean horizon. "America, get ready. We're on our way!"

Their joy didn't last long. Three hundred miles westward, the *Speedwell's* leaking worsened and could not be stopped. The captain said they simply could not go on. They returned to Plymouth, accompanied by the *Mayflower.* There, the *Speedwell* was pronounced unfit for ocean travel.

"What will we do?" Mother asked.

"Go on the *Mayflower,*" Father replied.

John and Sarah stared at each other. How long ago it seemed since John had longed to sail on the larger ship. Now it would happen. He could hardly wait! Then a disturbing thought entered his mind. "I heard the captain say she isn't built for so many people," he said.

"We have no choice," Father sternly told them. "It is already mid-September." Worry clouded his face. "If we had gone when we were supposed to, there would have been time to plant and harvest some winter crops. Instead, we've spent seven weeks on board ship so far, longer than the crossing itself should be.

"We've been forced to live in miserable conditions, cold and hungry and thirsty. Our food and fresh water supply have run low. People are sick. The crew is threatening to walk off. They say the emigrants interfere with their work, and in truth, some of them do."

"William, I have never seen you so discouraged." Mother placed her hand on Father's arm. Her forehead wrinkled with concern.

"I know. These are discouraging days." He sighed, his face troubled. "Decisions must be made. Now. Some of our people are turning back. Abigail, shall we go back to Leiden with them? Only about thirty of our group plan to continue."

"John and Sarah?" Mother turned to them.

John spoke first. "What you say is true, Father. There will be little or no chance of harvest in the New World. Yet suppose we stay? If we remain in England, Elder Brewster will be thrown into the dungeon, perhaps hanged for treason. So will others—perhaps even you." He fought the fear that rose inside him. "Life was not easy in Holland, and it isn't safe there anymore. I believe we should go on, but I will abide by whatever you and Mother decide."

"Sarah?"

She looked thin and small in her plain dress. Lack of proper food had left its mark on her childish face. John desperately wished he had money to buy Sarah all she needed. He saw her struggle with the question. Her green eyes changed expressions a dozen times before she said, "I miss Leiden and Gretchen and our home." She looked down at her fingers.

John held his breath, waiting for her to continue. Father and Mother would decide, but he wanted his sister to be happy.

"I miss them," Sarah repeated in a low voice. "But there isn't any home to go back to. We sold our house and most of our things. We have to go on. As long as we have each other. . ."

"That's right, Sarah. I'm proud of you. And you, too, John." Mother drew herself up to her full height, looking far taller than she really was. "William, for better or worse, we sail with the *Mayflower.*"

Father bowed his head and thanked God for his family, but not before John saw the look in his face and the shine of tears in his eyes.

Strangely enough, once those who'd decided to continue the journey moved to their cramped quarters aboard the *Mayflower,* their hopes rose.

Slowly, then with gathering speed, the *Mayflower* sailed away from England. John and Sarah watched England grow smaller and smaller, until it became only a speck in the distance. Even though they had never lived in England, their parents' stories had sunk deep into their hearts. John couldn't hold in his feelings when he saw slow tears spill from his parents' eyes.

"Good-bye, King James, you miserable wretch," he cried, loud enough so only Mother, Father, and Sarah could hear. Such talk was treason, and some of the London Strangers loyally followed the king and the Church of England. "I hope God punishes you for persecuting us just because we want to worship God in our own way!" He shook his fist at the retreating English shore.

"John!" Sarah's horrified gasp made him realize what he'd done.

"That is quite enough." Father's arms shot out. His hands fastened on John's shoulders, and he sternly looked at his son. "Never call down God's punishment on anyone. It is a terrible thing to do."

"Not even when they deserve it?"

The hint of a smile came to Father's lips but disappeared

so quickly John wondered if it had been there at all. "Nay, lad. God deals with all of us in His own time, in His own way."

"I didn't mean to say it out loud," John explained. "The words just came."

"It's just as bad to think wicked things as to speak them," Mother quietly said. "Remember the Scripture, 'For as he thinketh in his heart, so is he.' John, you *must* learn to hold that tongue of yours! It will get you into trouble again and again." She shook her head. "Soon you will be a man. I fear for you. If you do not put away childish habits and learn to control your temper, how can you be a witness for the Master?" She sadly shook her head.

John bit his lip. He hated himself when he did something wrong and made Mother look like that. He glanced at Sarah. She stood with arms crossed and a worried expression on her face much like Mother's, except it also held sympathy. John knew how tenderhearted she was. Sarah hurt as much as John when Father or Mother had to correct or punish him. She had also kept him out of trouble many times by not telling their parents of his mischief—including the incident with Klaus. Dr. Fuller also had remained silent after getting John's promise that he would be more careful of what he said and did in the future.

Now John had failed again. "I'm sorry," he mumbled. "I'll try to do better."

"You are forgiven." Father's hold on John tightened before his strong arms fell to his sides. The twinkle John thought he had seen a moment before returned and grew. "I confess, there have been times when I have felt the same way about King James and his men!"

"You?" John rocked back on his heels. His mouth dropped open.

"Aye. Then I remember that we are to forgive our enemies as our Father in heaven forgives us." He smiled at the children, took Mother's arm, and led her away, leaving John and Sarah to stare after them in wonder.

Shocked by Father's confession, John unthinkingly leaned against the ship's rail. He failed to hear heavy steps pounding down the deck until Sarah gave a small warning cry of alarm. John turned, straight into two powerful, hairy arms!

CHAPTER 8

Pilgrims, Strangers, and Sailors

"How many times d' you gotta be told to stay away from that rail?" the sailor hissed. He yanked John back from the rail with such force the boy spun across the deck and landed on a pile of coiled rope! John lay still for a moment, unhurt but stunned by the unexpected attack. Sarah ran to him on flying feet. "Are you hurt?"

"No." Good intentions to stay out of trouble vanished. John leaped up, brushed his sister aside, and sprang to face the cowardly attacker who had jumped him from behind. The next instant, astonishment filled him.

"Why, it's—" His jaw dropped.

Sarah had recovered her wits enough to join her brother. "Mr. Klaus, whatever are you doing on the *Mayflower?*" she asked, pleasure lighting up her face.

Klaus grimly folded his arms across his brawny chest and continued to glower. "My name ain't Mister an' 'tis a good thing fer you that I be aboard," he sourly stated. "What'd I tell you about leanin' on that rail?"

"I forgot." John's delight at seeing the sailor again overcame fear.

Klaus rudely snorted. "Better not be fergettin' when I'm around. I ain't fishin' no more brats outta the drink, y' hear me?" He scowled even more.

"How did you get here?" John persisted. "Sarah and I looked for you before the *Speedwell* left for London. William Bradford said it would be sold and go back to being a cargo ship, instead of trying to carry passengers."

"Aye," Klaus grunted. He heaved his wide shoulders into a shrug. "I've sailed the seven seas but ain't seen the New World. All the jaw-flappin' about it gave me a hankerin' t' see wi' my own eyes." He raised a shaggy eyebrow. "Got released from the *Speedwell* an' signed on this'un." Klaus threw out his chest with pride. "Ain't no better sailor on board. Cap'n was glad t' get me."

A gleam in his eyes showed how proud Klaus was of being a good sailor. John also suspected he and Sarah had something to do with the big seaman's decision to change ships.

He wisely held his tongue. Such a remark would surely bring back the scowl Klaus usually wore that had slipped away during their conversation.

"We're glad you're going with us," Sarah politely said.

Klaus reached out a calloused hand, as if to touch her hair, then snatched it back. The scowl returned. "Some'un's gotta look atter the pair o' you," he muttered. "Ain't gonna be me, though." He wheeled and strode away without a backward glance.

"Well, I never!" Sarah indignantly said. "Why can't he be

friendly?" She tilted her freckled nose and said in an exact imitation of the newcomer to the *Mayflower,* " 'Some'un's gotta look atter the pair o' you. Ain't gonna be me, though!' Who asked him to look after us is what I want to know," she added in her normal voice.

John cocked his head. His eyes sparkled. "I'm glad he's here. Besides, remember what Dr. Fuller said. You just never know. I have a feeling that before we reach America, we may be mighty glad Klaus is on board." He made a face. "At least we have one friend among the crew. Most of the sailors hate us."

"You never did tell me why." Sarah trotted down the deck to keep up with her brother's longer stride. Her dark braids bounced.

"They don't like our prayers and hymns," John explained. "Also, some of the Pilgrims treat the sailors as if they are so ignorant they aren't worth anything except to keep the ship going. I wouldn't like to be treated that way."

"Perhaps that's why I overheard a sailor say he'd like to throw half of us into the sea," Sarah said. "Klaus said that to you, too, but I don't think he meant it."

"I don't, either." Suddenly John felt gloriously happy. Having Klaus with them made everything that much better. "If he got mad and threw me in, I'll wager he'd jump right in and fish me out, in spite of everything he says!"

"I do, too," Sarah giggled.

John went back to the subject of the sailors. "Do you know what they call us? 'Glib-gabbety puke stockings!' Just because our people get seasick. Isn't that awful?"

Sarah stopped and put her hands on her hips. "It's terrible. What right do they have to call us names? The sailors curse and use bad language, even in front of our women!"

"Once they get us safely to the New World, they'll load the *Mayflower* with cargo and sail back to England," John told her. "I wish Klaus would stay with us, but he probably wouldn't make a very good landlubber."

Sarah gave a peal of laughter. "Landlubber! You're beginning to sound like a sailor, John Smythe." She danced around in front of him, grinning. "Avast, me hearties, 'tis a sail I see."

"If Mother hears you talking like that, she'll wash your mouth out with soap," John warned, but he couldn't help laughing. It was good to see Sarah happy. Most of the time Mother kept Sarah close beside her, unwilling for her daughter to be around the rough sailors.

John and Sarah soon made friends with the other children aboard, not only with the older children from Leiden, but also with the servants and children of the Strangers. They had to make their own fun. Sometimes it was watching the sailors, making sure to keep out of their way. At other times, they played with the few dogs aboard or with the ship's cat.

Sarah liked to read the books William Brewster had brought, even if they were grown-up books.

John didn't. "Why spend time reading when there is so much to learn?" he demanded. He explored all of the ship he could without getting into trouble. Anything to keep out of the damp, unpleasant sleeping quarters that held most of the passengers!

Captain Christopher Jones had moved to a small cabin so that about twenty of the persons he considered most important could sleep in his quarters. A few slept in a small shallop that would be used to explore the rivers of the New World. The rest of the passengers were crammed into the space below the main deck. The room was dim and nearly airless. Everyone slept on the floor. John longed to sleep topside with the sailors, but he had to stay with his family.

People wore the same clothes day after day. They put on everything they owned to keep from freezing in their unheated quarters. With only the salty seawater to wash themselves in, it was impossible to keep clean. Soon the smell of unwashed bodies and unwashed clothes became overpowering. When people became sick, the smell grew even worse. Could anyone stand it for two long months? The Pilgrims gritted their teeth and held on. So did the Strangers.

John amused himself by learning as much as he could about his fellow travelers and passing his new knowledge on to his family. "Myles Standish is going to be our captain when we reach America," he reported. "He is to lead us in defending ourselves against unfriendly Indians."

"Why him?" Sarah wanted to know. She gave a little shiver. "I know it's wrong not to like people, but he looks so mean! I wonder if his wife, Rose, is happy."

"Would you be if you were married to him?" John teased.

"No sir!" Sarah shook her head. "Why can't Mr. Alden be

our captain? I like him a lot. He's always so polite and calls me Mistress Smythe." She held both sides of her skirt wide and curtsied.

"John Alden is a cooper, not a soldier," Father reminded the children. "He will be kept busy making and repairing barrels, as he has done here on the *Mayflower*."

"We must be fair," Mother put in. "I've heard Mr. Standish is brave and fearless. If there is trouble with the Indians—and I pray to God there will be none—we will need an experienced soldier."

John laughed. "Do you want to hear something funny? I heard a man say of him, 'A little chimney is soon fired.'"

"What does that mean?" Sarah eagerly leaned forward.

"Whoever made the unkind remark means Myles Standish is not only short but has a bad temper that flares up quickly," Father said. "I hope, son, you will repeat it to no one else."

"I won't," John promised.

Another day he announced, "I think John Alden admires Priscilla Mullins."

"I knew that before we left England," Sarah boasted. "I can see why, too. She is friendly and nice."

"Miss Mullins is indeed a good girl," Mother agreed. "Although she is only eighteen, she has proved to be a hard worker. She helps the mothers who have small children and also does more than her share of the cooking." A smile tipped her lips upward. "That is, when we are allowed to cook. It is so discouraging to have rain and waves splash water into our living space! Hard biscuits and salted beef or pork are not proper food."

"The sailors call the biscuits hardtack and the salted meat salt horse," John said. "I like hot food better."

"I hate picking bugs out of my food worst of all," Sarah complained.

"Better than leaving them in and eating them!" John laughed at the expression on his sister's face.

Sometimes even John found the wide Atlantic Ocean a lonely place. Questions raced through his busy mind. It was dangerous for a ship to make the crossing by herself. Suppose they were shipwrecked. No one would ever know. What if they ran out of food? They could starve, just as others had done before them.

So far, there had been no sign of pirates. John felt thankful. He hadn't repeated to Sarah the bloodcurdling stories he had teased Klaus into telling him when the sailor was off duty and not sleeping. Names like buccaneers, freebooters, and sea rovers danced in John's head. He suspected Klaus stretched his stories. Still, the wicked-looking scar on the sailor's shoulder supported his tales.

Klaus still scowled, but John knew the rough sailor liked him. "All because I didn't tell the captain of the *Speedwell* what happened that day," John muttered to himself. "I'm glad I didn't." He shivered, thinking of the dreaded cat-o'-nine-tails. Just thinking of those cords lashing a man's back made John feel sick.

Fortunately, there had been no whippings aboard the *Mayflower*, at least so far.

John prayed there never would be.

CHAPTER 9

Storm at Sea

Raging winds moaned and howled like screaming, hungry beasts. Day and night the roaring sea battered the *Mayflower* without letting up. She rolled and pitched. Her timbers creaked and groaned like someone in pain. With each new attack, it seemed the gallant ship must burst apart at the seams. Captain Jones and his crew fought the storm with all their might, as they had fought many others. Yet in spite of their best efforts, they could barely keep the ship from going down with all her passengers.

Mothers hugged their small children, trying to protect them from the wind and waves. People clung to whatever was fastened down in order to keep from being swept into the sea.

John was greatly disappointed that Father would not allow him to go topside during the worst of the storm.

"It's too dangerous," Father said. "If someone doesn't fall overboard before this storm ends, it will only be by the grace of God."

His words planted a seed of fear in John's heart. It was bad enough being cooped up with so many people. What must it be like on deck? "What about Klaus and the other sailors?" he anxiously asked.

"They have sailed stormy seas many times," Father reassured him. "They know what to do and how to protect themselves."

That made John feel better. Surely a seaman such as his rough friend who had faced pirates and escaped with only a badly cut shoulder could beat a storm.

John swallowed his fear and tried to comfort Sarah, pale-faced and sick from the heaving ship. "Don't worry. The ballast in the bottom of the *Mayflower* will keep her upright when the strong winds hit the sails. So will the cargo below the passenger deck."

A wild cry arose, loud enough to be heard even above the storm. "The seams! The winds have forced open the deck seams!" The next moment, a wave of icy seawater poured down onto the sick and frightened travelers, drenching them from head to foot. It soaked blankets and food. The terrified little band huddled together, seeking comfort as much as warmth.

Just when everyone felt they would surely die in the storm, William Brewster's voice rolled out. "Brethren, be of good cheer! Have we not been told the same God we worship and for whom we have abandoned our homes is the God of the sea? Remember the words of the Psalmist: 'The Lord said, I will bring my people again from the depths of the sea.' Did God not part the waters of the Red Sea long ago and bring His children safely through?"

Dripping wet, teeth chattering from his freezing bath, Elder Brewster stood among his flock and offered encouragement in the very face of death!

Elder Brewster went on. "Let us pray. Almighty Father, God of land and sea and sky, have mercy on us. If it be Thy will for us to reach America, build a colony, and worship Thee, deliver us from this raging storm. If it be Thy will to take us even unto Thyself, so be it. We are Thy children, and Thou art our Father. We are in Thy hands. Forgive our trespasses and make us—"

C-r-a-c-k. The sound of something breaking cut off Elder Brewster's prayer.

"What was *that?*" Sarah cried.

"I don't know." Father staggered to his feet, hung onto whatever he could, and prepared to investigate.

John sprang up. "May I come?"

"No!" Father's voice sharpened with fear. "Stay with Mother and Sarah!"

John dropped back to the pile of soaked blankets, wishing Father would realize he was man enough to go along at such times. *Perhaps he would, if you didn't get into mischief and acted more like a man,* a little voice inside reminded him.

Father returned in a very few minutes. "I have bad news. The main beam has cracked. The deck is in splinters."

"How could such a huge beam crack?" John demanded, not believing what his ears had just heard.

"A beam can stand only so much strain," Father replied.

"Is the *Mayflower* going to sink?" Sarah whispered. She scooted closer to her mother.

"We hope not." Father's calm voice made his daughter feel better. "We are in God's hands, as Elder Brewster said."

A cold, wet hand crept into John's. Sarah's lips trembled.

Her face was so white freckles stood out like thick stars on a cloudless night.

If only he could do something to make her feel better! John quickly thought how his sister cheered up when he said something funny. He shook his head. Nothing was funny about either the storm or having the main beam of their ship cracked.

Maybe a verse of Scripture would help. John frantically ran through some of those he'd learned in meeting until he came to one that brought a grin to his cold, blue lips. "Sarah, remember how Elder Brewster is always saying all things work together for good to them that love God?"

A spark of interest crept into her frightened eyes. "Yes, but I don't see any good now."

"There is, though. You know our clothes are dirty from all this time we've worn them. Well, the sea just washed them for us, didn't it?" John knew how weak his joke was, but he couldn't think of anything else, and he couldn't bear to see Sarah so miserable. He felt warmth steal into his chilled body when Father sent him a grateful look.

"That's right, John! Thank you for reminding us," Father said.

"Can they fix the beam?" Mother asked anxiously.

"I'm not sure. It may mean we will have to turn back to England." Father sounded sad.

"Turn back! When we're already halfway there?" John felt his old spirit return. "There must be a way to fix the beam." He raised his head. "Listen. The howl of the storm is not quite so strong."

"Thank God for that." Father started back topside. Before John could ask permission, Father said, "You may come along, son, but hang on to me at all times. The storm still rages."

When they reached the deck, John's mouth fell open. Shivers chased up and down his spine—and not just from his wet clothing. The deck had been splintered. A great crack in the main beam clearly showed how badly it had been damaged.

Captain Jones stood nearby, talking with a few men, including John Howland. The Smythes liked the hearty young man, a servant to John Carver.

"Recaulking the seams is no problem," Captain Jones stated. "But we must repair the buckled main beam."

"We cannot do that unless we go back to England," a man said.

Jones crossed his arms over his chest and stubbornly replied, "My ship is strong and firm beneath the water line. Once we get the main beam fixed, there is no need to turn back."

The arguing went on. Suddenly a great gust of wind rocked the *Mayflower*. Father wrapped his arms around John, braced himself, and shouted in John's ear, "We must go below again!" Before they could move, a great wave swept John Howland across the deck, over the rail, and into the churning sea!

"Man overboard!" The cry burst from a dozen throats.

John's heart missed a beat then pounded with the same fury as the increasing storm. No one could live in those waves!

A great cheer rose above the roaring of the storm.

"What is it?" John yelled.

"The lad's grabbed ahold o' a topsail halyard!" Klaus

bellowed. Carrying a boat hook, the sailor headed toward the ship's rail at a dead run. He leaped obstacles and swept aside two of his fellow seamen when the pitch of the ship threw them into his path.

"It's a miracle!" a Pilgrim shouted.

"A miracle?" John cried, gazing on the line that hung overboard and ran out at length. There was no sign of John Howland. "He must be deep under the water!"

"He's holding on," Klaus bellowed. A few moments later, the big sailor used his boat hook and hauled Howland to safety, brawny arms straining. For the second time the seaman had cheated the angry waters of a victim.

Scared and soaked, Howland wordlessly gripped his rescuer's hand. Another cheer rose.

The winds died down a little. Or perhaps they were only gathering for another assault on the shaken, leaky *Mayflower*. The near-tragedy had taken attention away from the crippled ship, but now discussions began again.

"A great iron screw was loaded wi' the Pilgrims' goods," a sailor volunteered.

"Why would they be taking an iron screw to America?" Captain Jones barked. "It ain't a normal piece of baggage!"

"Aye, aye, sir. Mebbe that God o' their'n knew we'd need it." The sailor slapped his leg and laughed. Others joined in.

"Silence!" Jones roared. "Klaus, get that screw, if there is such a thing. With a post under it, the job can be done."

At Father's insistence, John unwillingly went below again. He wanted to see the crew raise the great screw and mend the beam. He wanted to tell Klaus how proud he was of him. Instead he had to content himself with reporting the excitement to Mother and Sarah.

"Klaus could have been washed into the sea, just like John Howland," he said breathlessly. "He is so brave. Klaus hauled John in the same way he'd haul in a huge fish. The sea tugged and pulled, as if it didn't want to give Howland up. I saw it with my own eyes, Sarah!"

Once the main beam was repaired, the *Mayflower* sailed on. John's curiosity burned brighter than ever. One day he asked William Bradford, "Did God really cause us to bring the great iron screw? Did He know the beam would crack? And that if there hadn't been a screw, we would have had to go back?"

Bradford shook his head. "Perhaps." Deep trouble showed in his eyes. John knew why and felt sorry for him. William's frail wife, Dorothy, had not been able to bear the miserable living conditions on shipboard as well as the others. She grew paler and sadder each day. The Smythes feared she would never live to reach the New World. Would the grieving woman die at sea, without ever seeing her little son, John, who had been left behind?

John wished he hadn't bothered William Bradford. He slipped away by himself, needing time to think. Why was life so hard? Why did God allow terrible storms to come, when the Pilgrims only wanted to get to America where they could serve Him? John looked out across the water, peaceful for a change. "You treacherous sea," he cried. "You look so smooth, but all the time you're getting ready to beat against us again and again. Well, you're not going to win! You hear? God's going to help us get to America, in spite of you."

John shook his fist at the calm ocean, but shivered. What would happen next?

CHAPTER 10

Where Did Everyone Go?

One of the children's favorite things to do when weather permitted them to be on the top deck was to watch the barefoot crew at work. John would have given anything to be able to climb up and down the rigging like monkeys scrambling up and down trees in a forest. Time after time he considered it, but the threatening looks he got from the sailors dampened his enthusiasm. Besides, after his experiences during the storm, John was trying harder than ever to stay out of trouble.

"I don't have to worry about you so much now," Sarah observed one day. "I'm glad." She sighed. "John, everyone talks about whether we should go on or turn back."

"What do you want to do?" he asked her.

She stared at him from dark-circled eyes. "I'm too tired to care. I just wish we'd get somewhere. Anywhere. I'm so tired of the winds. Tired of the ship rising and falling and making so many people ill. Most of all, I'm tired of helping Mother care for the sick. I know I shouldn't feel that way, but all I want to do is drop down in a heap and sleep."

"Poor Sarah." John gently pulled one of her braids. "Lie down and rest for a little while. I'll take your place."

"You can't help the women, and more of them are sick than the men."

"If you don't rest, you'll be sick yourself," he argued.

Sarah gave in and curled up on the damp deck. John heaped blankets around her until only her green eyes and the top of her head showed. "There. Rest now."

"John, I feel so strange. It's like we left Holland years ago—not just a few weeks. Sometimes I can't even remember what it was like there. All I can think of is the ocean and the storms." Tears came. "I wonder if Gretchen ever thinks of me. I wonder if—" Her voice trailed off.

John stayed with Sarah until she drifted into a restless sleep. "I'm glad I'm not a girl," he whispered to himself. "It is so much harder for her." He searched his brain for a way to make his sister feel better. At last he came up with a plan and put it into action a few days later.

The pitching ship had steadied, at least for a time. People began to feel better. They gathered in the weak, late autumn sunshine, well wrapped against the cold air. The Pilgrims prayed, sang hymns, and talked about America.

"Tell us more about the New World," John begged a weathered traveler known for his interesting stories. All the children on board liked hearing them whenever time allowed them to gather around the old man.

"Shall I tell you about the Lost Colony?" the old man asked.

"Yes! Yes!" the children cried.

Sarah perked up enough to ask, "How could a colony get lost?" A bit of color came to her thin cheeks and spread beneath her freckles. Her eyes sparkled.

John gave a sigh of relief. His plan was working!

"It's a curious story, and it happened way back in 1585," the storyteller began in a mysterious voice. "Sir Walter Raleigh, you all know who he is?"

"Oh, yes," they chorused. John added, "A soldier, writer, and explorer."

Priscilla Mullins, who stood a little way from the children, called, "There's a story about him meeting Queen Elizabeth. It may not be true, but people say she was out walking and stopped by a huge mud puddle. According to the story, Sir Walter Raleigh took off his coat, threw it in the mud puddle, and made a dry place for her to walk across."

"That's funny!" the children shouted.

"It's silly," eight-year-old Francis Billington announced. He and his brother, sons of Strangers John and Eleanor Billington, were troublemakers. Any mischief on board the *Mayflower* found them in the middle of it, and the Smythe children tried to stay as far away from them as possible.

"I wouldn't put my coat in the mud, even for the queen," John Billington said.

"It may never have happened," the old man laughed. "What did happen was that Raleigh became Queen Elizabeth's favorite. She gave him a twelve-thousand-acre estate in Ireland, where he planted the first potatoes. British explorers brought potatoes to England and Ireland from South America."

"What about the Lost Colony?" Francis demanded.

"I'm getting to that, young 'un. Raleigh sent a band of about one hundred men to settle in America in a place called Virginia. They dug themselves in offshore on an island called Roanoke, but they had a mighty thin time of it.

" 'Bout a year later, they sailed back to England. More colonists came, bringing supplies and stuff to trade with the Indians. All but fifteen of them also went back, according to the story. Then another bunch came. This time there were women and children among them. The sailors dumped them on Roanoke Island, but you know what?" The old man's eyes glistened.

"What?"

John looked at Sarah. She leaned forward, as eager to hear as the others.

"When the next batch came, there wasn't hide nor hair of those who had stayed in America!"

"Where did they go?" a half-dozen voices cried, Sarah's among them.

The old man shook his head. "No one knows."

"Someone has to know," John Billington scoffed.

"They don't, and the story gets even curiouser. About a month after the group that had women and children came to Roanoke, the first English child was born in America. She was John White's granddaughter, and they called her Virginia Dare." John suspected the storyteller was enjoying his tale as much or more than those who listened!

"White didn't want to leave, but the colony badly needed supplies. He sailed to England." Excitement lighted the old man's face. "War came with Spain. England couldn't and wouldn't give White supplies or a ship. He had to wait before he could sail back to America."

"And he didn't find anyone? Not even his granddaughter?" Sarah burst out.

"Right you are, little lady. All he and those with him found were the letters *CRO* carved on one tree and the word *Croatan* on another."

"But that's impossible! How could they just vanish?" John asked.

"I said it was curious, didn't I?" The storyteller's eyes twinkled, but a look of awe lurked in their depths. "Some say they must have been captured and carried off by unfriendly Indians. Others say that ain't so at all. They hold that when the colonists ran out of food, they joined a friendly tribe called *Croatans* and left the name on the tree to show folks where they were. Still others said they must have gone away to find food.

"Like I said, there wasn't hide nor hair of any of them, not even little Virginia Dare. No one knows and no one ever will know where those folks disappeared to after the ship sailed back to England."

"That is so sad." Sarah's eyes looked like saucers.

Maybe the story hadn't been such a good idea after all, John miserably thought. He knew as long as he lived, he'd remember the Lost Colony and little Virginia Dare. He'd just bet Sarah would, too. His mouth felt dry. His eyes burned. What kind of country were they going to, that swallowed people and left no trace but a few letters and a mysterious word carved on a tree?

CHAPTER 11

What Happened to All the Food?

Sarah Smythe wearily trudged down the deck of the *May-flower*. Her stomach growled. She quickly looked both ways. No one was close enough to hear except the ship's cat. Thank goodness for that. It was so embarrassing when her complaining stomach got so loud others could hear!

"I don't know why it should bother me," Sarah told the cat, who lay curled on top of a coil of heavy rope. "Everyone else's stomach is growling, too."

The cat yawned, looking bored.

"A lot you care." Sarah resentfully eyed the animal's well-fed body. "You can catch your dinner. The rest of us have to put up with moldy cheese, hardtack so dried out it has to be soaked before anyone can eat it, and bad butter!" Her stomach grew queasy at the thought of the unappetizing meals.

"What's wrong, little sister?" John said from behind her.

"I'm so hungry, I'm about ready to start in on him!" Sarah pointed at the cat and took a step toward him.

The sudden movement sent the cat into the air, fur standing

straight up. He came down on all four feet, gave Sarah a baleful look, and streaked down the deck. His angry *meowrrr* split the calm air and brought peals of laughter from the Smythes.

"Do you think he understood me?" Sarah said, when she could get her breath.

John let out a whoop. "I don't know, but he was taking no chances!"

"That he wasn't," a new voice agreed. A broadly grinning Klaus paused for a moment on his way aft. "That ol' cat lit out 's if a banshee were atter him."

"What's a banshee?" Sarah wanted to know.

John wiped tears from his eyes. "A make-believe creature that wails and howls, right, Klaus?"

"Aye, lad. But I dunno 'bout the make-b'lieve part." His shaggy eyebrows met over his eyes.

"Have you ever seen a banshee?"

Klaus shook his head. "Naw, but I kin hear 'em howlin' in the wind." He went on his way, leaving John and Sarah staring after him, then at each other.

"There aren't really banshees, are there?" Sarah pulled her warm cloak closer around her shivering body.

"No. They're something somebody made up, perhaps to frighten children." John grinned at her.

Sarah's stomach growled again, louder this time.

John's eyes opened wide. He threw one hand against his heart in mock fear. "Is that a banshee I hear? Maybe Klaus is right, after all!"

John's laughter brought stinging tears to Sarah's eyes. Her

usual good nature disappeared. "Can't you ever be serious about anything?" she cried. Red flags of color waved in her thin cheeks. "John Smythe, your own sister is so hungry she's jealous of a ship's cat, and you stand there laughing!"

"I can't help it," John choked out. "You don't want rats or mice for dinner, do you? They wouldn't be cooked, of course—"

Sarah's already churning stomach couldn't stand the thought of eating rodents. In spite of Klaus and his warnings, she headed for the ship's rail.

"Sarah, I'm sorry!" John sounded miserable. He hung onto his sister until what little food she had in her came up then led her to a deserted spot that was sheltered a bit from the wind. "I was only trying to make you laugh."

Sarah ducked her head and stared at the deck. "I know." She wiped tears from her face with the back of her none-too-clean hand. "It's just that we go on and on and seem to get nowhere. The food is almost gone. What will we do if we run out of things to eat before we get to America?"

The question hung heavy in the air. John finally said without much conviction, "Well, God sent manna to the children of Israel. He could do it again, I s'pose."

His weak attempt to make Sarah feel better brought a half-smile. She closed her eyes and said, "Remember all the food that got loaded into the hold of the *Mayflower?*"

"How could I forget?" John snorted. "We laughed and told each other there was enough food to take us all around the world, not just to America."

"Where did it all go?" Sarah wondered. She opened her

eyes. "I can still see the crates and crates of vegetables, lemons, and limes." Her mouth watered. "How I'd like to have some of them now!"

"So would I." John joined in the game. "It seems impossible we could eat so many sacks of flour, potatoes, dried beans, and peas. Or that all the barrels of salted-down pork and beef, the slabs of bacon, and jars of oil are nearly used up.

"Too bad we don't have a barrel of grain and a small bottle of oil like the widow who fed Elijah." Sarah sighed and fell silent, thinking of the story from the Bible. "John, if you were like the widow and only had enough meal and oil to make one little cake for us, would you give it to a stranger who asked for food? Even though it meant we would starve?"

John cocked his head to one side. Sarah could see how seriously he took her question. After a few moments he said, "It would depend on the stranger. Elijah was so close to God, it must have shown in the way he acted. Remember, Elijah told the woman not to be afraid. He also promised if she would make him a little cake, the food would never run out until the Lord sent rain and the crops would grow."

Sarah felt her heart beat faster. "Do you think the widow knew Elijah was a prophet of God?"

"She must have had faith in him, or she wouldn't have given away the food her son needed. I might give away my own food, but I'm not sure I'd give away yours or Father's or Mother's."

"It's a good thing the widow believed what Elijah said," Sarah soberly told her brother. "She always had enough to feed her son, herself, and the prophet." Sarah's empty stomach grumbled again. "Oh, dear! How can I wait until it's time for the next meal?"

John leaped up the same way the ship's cat had done earlier. "Stay here. I'll see if I can get you something."

Sarah watched him head aft, racing along at top speed. What did he have in mind? With the food supply almost gone, how could he find anything for her poor stomach? There simply was not enough food on board for people to eat between meals.

A dull ache settled in her middle. She watched the rolling waves. "Father, thank You they aren't so high now," she prayed in a whisper. She mustn't get sick again. Mother had enough to do caring for those who were already sick. Shame filled Sarah's heart. "I'm sorry to complain, God. Please, help us get to America safely."

She thought of the wonderful stories of the New World. Fruit and nut trees. Deer in the forests and no king to say hungry people must not kill and eat them. Fish—so many all one had to do was put in a net and bring in a great haul.

Still thinking of the good things to eat they would have in America, Sarah grew drowsy. A hand shaking her shoulder roused her from the daydream that had changed into a dream of summer skies, ripe fruit, and laughing children.

"Wake up, Sarah," someone whispered.

She opened her eyes.

John huddled on the deck before her, his back to some passengers who had come topside to take advantage of the calmer weather. "Shh. Don't let anyone see," he warned.

Sarah stared at the small piece of dried beef in her brother's hand. Her mind whirled. Alarm rose inside her. "John, where did you get this? You didn't *steal* it, did you?"

"Don't be a goose," he scornfully told her. "Besides being wrong, stealing food when supplies are so low would bring a terrible punishment."

He handed the meat to Sarah. She saw the hunger in his eyes but knew he hadn't taken one morsel. "Do you have a knife?"

John licked his lips but shook his head. "You need it worse than I do." No amount of persuasion could talk him into sharing the meat.

Her mouth filled with the hard stuff, Sarah said between chewing, "You still haven't told me how and where you got it."

John shrugged, but his eyes sparkled. "What would you say if I said I told Klaus you were so hungry you'd considered eating the ship's cat?"

"You didn't!" Sarah gasped. A little stream of juice trickled from her lips. "You know I wasn't serious. What will he think of me? John, how could you?"

"Shh," John warned again. He quickly wiped the telltale drops away. "I didn't say I told him." His mischievous brown eyes glowed with the excitement of fooling his sister. "I just asked—"

"I know what you asked." She clutched the tiny remaining piece of beef in one hand and glared at him. "Did you or did you not tell him?"

"I didn't." When Sarah drooped with relief, John added, "I only said you were most awf'ly hungry."

Curiosity overcame even hunger. "What did he do?"

"He ordered me to stay on deck." John's eyes flashed with admiration. "A few minutes later he came back with the dried beef."

"What did he say?" Visions of the punishment John had mentioned danced in Sarah's head. "Oh, dear, I hope Klaus didn't steal it!"

John hunched closer. His eyes darkened to the color of the ocean when storm clouds raced above. "He didn't. He has been hoarding the piece of meat for himself. But don't try to thank him. I already told him you would be grateful, and it's best to make sure no one knows about this."

"Even Father and Mother?" Sarah felt guilty already. Yet was it wrong to protect someone who had been kind?

"The more persons who know about it, the greater the chance that Klaus will get into trouble. People might assume that he'd stolen the meat," John reminded her.

Sarah swallowed the last salty bite. "At least my stomach has stopped growling."

"Good thing." John became his usual self. "There for awhile I was afraid Captain Jones might think someone set off a cannon!"

This time his teasing didn't bother her. Sarah giggled. "Or that a thunderstorm is coming close." She saw by John's grin how relieved he felt that her own storm had passed, at least for now.

"I know something fun to do." John sprang to his feet. "Let's go look at the chests of things going to the New World.

It will help us forget being hungry."

"Why?" Sarah asked. "What's the fun of looking at chests so tightly closed we can't open them—and wouldn't dare, if we could!"

"We can thump on them," John suggested. "We can try to guess all the things inside of them." His hair blew in the wind that had started to rise.

"All right." Sarah got up and followed him to where the chests holding everything imaginable sat fastened down so securely that not even the wildest waves could snatch and hurl them into the stormy ocean depths.

CHAPTER 12

Mischief on the *Mayflower*

John, Sarah, and a few other children, including the trouble-making Billington boys, daringly thumped on the top of the chests.

"This one sounds empty," Francis Billington complained, thumping away on the top.

"It prob'ly just had blankets and clothes. People took 'em out to keep from freezing," his brother John said.

John Billington thumped on another chest. "Wonder which ones have the trinkets?" He tried to shake the heavy trunk but couldn't budge it. "We hadta haul all this stuff from England just to trade with the stupid Indians."

"How do you know Indians are stupid?" John Smythe demanded.

"They must be, to want a bunch of glass beads, mirrors, cloth, and junk like that." Francis Billington stuck out his tongue and made an awful face.

"You can trade an iron pot for furs," John reminded him.

"I'll bet I could get a lot more furs from trading a musket than an old iron pot," Francis bragged. "All they have are bows and arrows. Bang. Bang, bang!" He raised an imaginary gun to his shoulder and pretended to squint along its barrel. "I'm gonna kill me a hundred Indians, maybe a thousand. I'm gonna be the greatest Indian-killer in the world."

"No, you aren't. I am!" John Billington pitched into Francis and they fell to the deck.

"Are not!" Francis squealed, arms waving wildly.

"Am too!" John howled when his brother's fist hit his eye.

"Stop that fighting this instant," a stern voice commanded. Captain Jones yanked the Billingtons up by the scruff of their necks and shook them hard. "Now get below, all of you!"

Sarah saw her brother's mouth open to protest. She grabbed his arm and hurried him away. The glint in the captain's steely eyes meant trouble.

"We weren't doing anything wrong," John protested.

"The Billingtons were, and we were with them," Sarah answered.

"They are always doing something wrong," John grumbled.

"I know." She felt a smile creep over her face. "At least they got caught this time and couldn't put the blame on someone else, the way they usually do."

"I can tell you what will happen," John said. "One of these times the Billingtons are going to do something so bad the captain will whale the living daylights out of them. They deserve it."

"John Smythe, watch what you say. Father will punish you if he hears you talking like that!" Sarah cried.

John stubbornly planted his feet on the deck and declared in imitation of Klaus, "Mark my words. You'll see what happens."

"You act like you want them to get in trouble." Sarah stared at her brother. "Would you like for people to feel that way about you?"

John didn't give an inch. "I only do funny things and play tricks. I don't do things that are dangerous or could hurt people."

"I know, but you worry Father and Mother and me. Not so much anymore," she loyally added. "It's probably because you're almost a man. You must have grown an inch since we left Leiden."

"You think so?" John looked pleased, and the subject of the Billingtons was dropped—but not for long. Within a few days, a terrible thing happened.

John and Sarah had just come on deck when they saw Francis Billington standing near some barrels of gunpowder.

"What's he doing?" Sarah whispered, craning her neck to see better.

"Probably nothing good." John's complaint turned to horror. "He has a musket. Sarah, get down!"

She fell to the deck, her terrified gaze fastened on Francis Billington.

"Stop that right now!" John roared, racing toward the eight-year-old boy.

Francis glanced around. A stubborn look settled on his face. "You can't tell me what to do." He pulled the trigger of the musket.

Boom!

The bitter smell of powder hung in the air. Men, women, and children came running. Sarah scrambled to her feet and raced toward the haze of smoke. "John, are you all right?" she asked.

"Yes, but—"

Klaus reached Francis Billington first. He caught him up in a grip of iron. "What were you thinking!" he roared. "Shootin' off a musket wi' kegs o' gunpowder near? Ain't there a brain in yer head? One spark coulda blown us t' bits! You should be fed t' the fishes, an' that brother o' yourn, too!" He dangled Francis above the deck and made as if to throw him overboard.

Francis, who had grinned broadly when the musket fired and people came running, tried to escape. His kicking legs only hit empty air. He tried to squirm free, fear written all over his dirty face—not for nearly blowing up the ship and all aboard including himself, but because of Klaus's scowling face and strong grip. Klaus marched closer and closer to the ship's rail.

A thrill of fear went through Sarah. "Don't let him do it," she begged John.

"He won't. He just wants to give Francis the scare of a lifetime," John whispered.

"Unhand my son, you miserable lout!" John Billington Sr. ran forward. "How dare you lay hands on an innocent child?" He faced Klaus. His fists were doubled, and his face was black with anger.

At his words, the watching crowd broke into cries of protest.

"Innocent, indeed!" a woman's voice rang out. "That 'innocent' child of yours shot off a musket next to the barrels of gunpowder and nearly sent us to the bottom of the sea!"

Billington's jaw dropped. "Is this true?" he demanded.

Francis, who still dangled like a puppet from Klaus's strong hand, couldn't say a word.

"He did, Papa! He did!" Young John Billington danced up and down in glee and clapped his hands over his brother's prank. "He made the gun go boom, and everyone came."

"Wait 'til I get my hands on you," Billington threatened Francis. "As for you, John Billington, get out of my sight, you sniveling talebearer!" He began to curse.

"That is quite enough of that language. There are ladies present," John Alden sternly reminded Mr. Billington. A murmur of agreement went through the crowd, and pretty Priscilla Mullins sent the young cooper a grateful look that made his eyes sparkle.

"Put the boy down, Klaus," Captain Jones ordered. "Not but what we'd all like to throw him overboard. It's what he deserves. Sir," he said, turning to Mr. Billington, "Never in all my sailing have I had the misfortune to have two such troublemakers on board as your sons. From now on, they are not to be on deck or anywhere else without you. I am holding you accountable for any further trouble," he added for good measure. "Is that clear?"

"There will be no more trouble," Mr. Billington promised. He made a grab for Francis, who managed to stay out of reach for a few moments. Mr. Billington soon caught his son. He carried the kicking, screaming boy below. Loud wails soon showed that the culprit was being punished for the latest of his sins.

"It is only by the grace and mercy of God that we have been saved this day," the Pilgrims said. They knelt on deck and thanked their heavenly Father for protecting them from an event that could so easily have ended in tragedy.

Sarah felt as limp as if she had fought a long, hard battle. "My goodness," she breathed to John after the crew returned to their duties and most of the passengers broke into little groups to discuss the latest near-disaster. "I would have thought even Francis Billington would know better than to do something like that."

"And he thinks the Indians are stupid!" John rolled his eyes.

"You were so brave, trying to stop him." Sarah felt proud of her big brother.

Instead of answering, John hung his head. His face turned white.

"John, are you sick?" Sarah asked, concern puckering her forehead.

He shook his head. After a moment, he said hoarsely, "Sarah, if I tell you something, will you promise not to repeat it to Father or Mother or anyone?"

"Do I ever repeat things you ask me not to tell?" she indignantly asked.

"No. You're a good secret-keeper." He cleared his throat. "It could have been me today instead of Francis."

"What do you mean?"

"I long to shoot a musket," John confessed. "Sometimes my fingers itch to take Father's out and try it." He stuffed his hands in his pocket. "Only the fear of Father's anger has kept me from doing so. Besides, we will need the powder when we get to America."

Fear worse than what she had felt when the musket had

been fired so close to those barrels of gunpowder dried Sarah's throat to a crisp. "Will we really, truly have to fight Indians?" she croaked.

John looked around to make sure no one could hear what he said. "I am afraid so. It all depends. Some Indians are friendly. Some are not."

"God says it is wrong to kill," Sarah whispered. Visions of terrible battles rose in her mind.

"I know." John stared out at the ocean. Sarah had the feeling he wasn't seeing water but instead was looking at a strange and unfriendly land peopled with natives who wanted no strangers among them.

He went on. "I know we must defend ourselves, but I don't think I could kill anyone." He brightened up. "Maybe if we trade with the Indians and treat them fairly, they will become our friends. Then we won't have to fight at all."

"I pray that will happen," Sarah softly told him. Her cold little hand touched his. "I don't want you to ever have to fight Indians."

"Let's talk about something else," John suggested. He got to his feet from where they'd been sitting on the deck. "We've had enough trouble for one day."

"All right." Sarah stood. "I know. Let's talk about the Hopkins family. I really like Constanta, Giles, and Damaris, don't you?" She anxiously added, "I'm afraid Mistress Hopkins can't wait until we reach America to have her new baby."

She laughed, and the joyous sound brought an answering smile to her brother's lips. "Mistress Hopkins told Mother that her husband, Stephen, says if the baby should be a boy and born on the *Mayflower*, they will name him Oceanus. Isn't that funny? Whoever heard of a baby named Oceanus?"

John chuckled and walked faster. Sarah pattered along beside him. "What if it's a girl?" he asked.

"I don't know." Sarah thought about it. "I suppose they could call her Oceana or maybe Atlanta for the sea. I still think they are funny names. Maybe they will change their minds." She slowed her steps. "John, it's been so hard on the women who are going to have babies. The storms, I mean. It's bad enough when you're feeling good, but Elizabeth Hopkins and Susanna White and Mary Collins must suffer so much more. They aren't getting the proper food."

Her heart ached with sympathy for the courageous mothers who had taken the chance of having to give birth at sea. "I hope their babies will be all right."

"I do, too," John mumbled. He scuffed his feet on the deck.

Sarah suspected he was just as worried about the women as she was but wouldn't say so.

A few days later, long after everyone had been asleep one night, Sarah roused to hear Dr. Fuller say, "Abigail, I need your help. Elizabeth's baby won't wait any longer to be born."

Wide-eyed and anxious, Sarah waited and prayed during the long night hours, heart thumping with fear. Would Mistress Hopkins and her new baby be all right?

CHAPTER 13

A Sad Day at Sea

Just before dawn, Sarah fell into a troubled sleep. In her dreams, it seemed she was back in Holland, running through the tulip fields with Gretchen. How bright and beautiful the flowers were: red and yellow, purple and white and pink. Thick green grass grew beneath a cloudless blue sky. Sarah's heart sang. The long voyage on the *Mayflower* must have been only a nightmare. It was so wonderful to be surrounded with color after all the gray ocean and sky and air.

The scene changed. "Hurry, Sarah," John called. "The canals are frozen deeply. Father says we may skate." The jingle of skates on his arm sang in her ears. She hastily put on heavy clothing, glad for the warmth. She had been cold for so long.

Her dream again changed. A small group sat around a long table on the large main floor of their meetinghouse, the Green Gate. Great quantities of steaming hot food covered the table—enough for everyone to eat their fill and some left to carry home. Sarah's mouth watered. Why had she never appreciated what she had? Pastor John Robinson offered a blessing for the meal. His wife, Bridget, and their three children sat next to him.

"Come, daughter. We must go to America," Father said. "Abigail. John. Come." He rose from his place at the table.

Sarah stared at him in horror. "America? Father, must we go? We haven't eaten, and I am so hungry! The ocean is wide and stormy and cold." She shivered and crossed her arms over her chest. "Please let us stay long enough to eat."

"There is no food," her father sadly told her.

She turned her gaze from him to the table. The feast had vanished. All that remained were scraps of moldy bread and cheese. A bright-eyed mouse leaped to the table and began to nibble on the unappetizing food. Sarah's stomach churned. She stood and backed away from the table.

"Come, Sarah." Mother gently shook her daughter's shoulder. "There is good news."

Good news! How could there be anything good when she was so hungry and cold?

"Sarah, open your eyes." This time John spoke.

She slowly obeyed. Father and Mother sat near her. John knelt beside her pallet on the damp floor. Understanding slowly dawned on her. Life on shipboard had not been the nightmare. She'd only dreamed of Holland with its tulips and skating, the feast that turned to crumbs. She was on the *Mayflower* and must have fallen asleep while praying for Elizabeth Hopkins.

Fear washed away her disappointment. She sat up and rubbed sleep from her eyes. "Is Mistress Hopkins all right?" she asked, almost afraid to hear the answer. "Did the baby come? Is it well?"

John interrupted her flow of questions. "That's the good news," he cried. "Mistress Hopkins and her brand new baby son are just fine!" Mischief danced in his eyes. He dropped his voice so others outside the family wouldn't hear. "They did name him Oceanus."

Sarah giggled. "He will probably be the only person in the whole world who is named that. I'm glad they are all right." A lump came to her throat. "I was afraid for them, so I prayed."

"As did we all," Father told her. His kind eyes smiled. "There will be a great deal of celebrating today."

Father was right. The baby's arrival renewed hope in the weary travelers with hungry stomachs and misery in their bones from the damp and cold.

"Just as Jesus was born in troublesome times, so has this baby been sent to us," Elder Brewster said. His thin, worn face glowed with happiness. "Oceanus Hopkins is a symbol of the new life we shall find in America. He will grow up in a land far from religious persecution. He shall be taught to worship God and read the Bible according to God's commands, not man's. No king shall dictate and demand obedience to what the child's conscience says is wrong."

Brewster's eyes glistened. Sarah felt mist rise to her own eyes. Her heart thrilled to the picture the elder painted.

Elder Brewster continued. "This child shall be free of fear. Think of it!" His voice rang with the old fire. "Oceanus will never be haunted by shadows of the dungeon and gallows. Praise God, he shall be free, even as we, who fled from England then sailed from Holland, are free!"

"Hurrah for Oceanus Hopkins!" John burst out, unable to keep still any longer.

"Hurrah!" Many took up the cry. For the first time in weeks, the fire that had filled hearts and souls before the Pilgrims left Holland spread over the faces of the weary Pilgrims. They burst into a spontaneous song of praise, thanking God for bringing them this far and asking His help for the rest of the voyage.

Yet just as the *Mayflower* itself went up and down with the force of the waves, so life on the ship had its ups and downs. One young sailor persecuted the Pilgrims. He never missed an opportunity to make fun of the sick people. He used as much bad language as possible, even in front of the women and children. Strong and conceited, he strode the deck, prancing over and around the sick and miserable Pilgrims.

"Fine lot ye are," he taunted. "Half of ye'll never make it." He grinned an evil grin. "Soon as yer bodies're heaved into the sea, I'll help meself to all ye brung with ye. I'd as soon throw half of ye in now."

When a few of the Pilgrims tried to reason with him, the sailor only bragged and blew, cursed and ridiculed them more. His ugly grinning face haunted the sick and made everyone feel worse. Only by the grace of God did the Pilgrims resist the temptation to throw their tormentor overboard.

Sarah knew how hard it was for John to hold his tongue. "He is no Klaus, grouchy outside and caring in his heart," she told her brother. "If you answer him back, that sailor might fling you into the sea." She shuddered at the thought. "Promise me you will stay away from him."

"I promise." John smiled at her. "I believe he's nothing but a dirty-mouthed braggart, but I wouldn't put it past him to carry out his threat—if he thought he could get away with it and hide what he did."

About halfway through the voyage, the sailor fell ill and died. William Bradford said, "Thus his curses light on his own head, and it is an astonishment to all his fellows for they note it to be the just hand of God upon him."

Other passengers agreed, and the superstitious crew wondered if such a fate might come to them if they persecuted the Pilgrims! The sailors kept as far away from the Pilgrims as possible for the rest of the journey, so the tired travelers didn't have to put up with as many insults.

"Do you *really* believe God made the sailor die because of what he did?" Sarah asked John. "What Mr. Bradford said makes me feel funny in here." She put her hand over her heart. "All of us do bad things. That's why Jesus came, so we could be forgiven for our sins. I don't like to think the God we pray to would kill someone just for being mean."

"William Bradford didn't say for sure that God killed the sailor," John explained. "He just said the man brought curses on his own head and that the rest of the crew believed God made it happen." He squirmed and admitted, "It makes me feel funny, too. Let's go ask Father and Mother."

Father considered their questions carefully. "It is not for us to know God's ways. Some see the tragedy as God's punishment. Others say the sailor would have become sick anyway."

He looked deep into his children's troubled eyes. "The important thing is to live every day in a way that is pleasing to our Master. That way, we will be ready to meet God when we die."

"You have to be sorry before your sins can be forgiven, don't you, Father?" Sarah asked. She leaned her head against his shoulder and looked into his face. John stood nearby.

"Yes, child." His hand smoothed her tangled braids and rested on her head for a moment. Shadows darkened Father's dark eyes.

"Do you think perhaps when the sailor got sick, he was sorry and asked God to forgive him?" John put in.

Father sadly shook his head. "I pray that he did. Sometimes people do call on God and ask for mercy just before they die. I fear the young sailor may not have been one of them, but only God knows for sure."

"I wish Klaus knew Jesus." John sighed. "I've tried to tell him, but he just says a God as great as ours wouldn't care about poor, miserable sailors."

To the children's surprise, Mother laughed. Her whole face lit up. "Son, the next time you have the chance to speak of the Lord to Klaus, ask him if he's ever heard of Peter, Andrew, James, and John."

"From the Bible?" Sarah wrinkled her forehead.

"That's it!" John shouted. "They were fishermen, too. Why didn't I think of that?" He disgustedly flopped down on the floor beside Sarah. "Jesus loved those men like brothers. He called them away from their fishing nets and made them His disciples. Wait 'til I tell Klaus!"

"Be careful that you don't rush at your sailor friend, sounding as if you know everything and he knows nothing," Father warned. "Pray for God to give you a chance to speak of His Son. In the meantime, Klaus will be watching to see if knowing Jesus has made any difference in your lives."

"How can we show that?" Sarah wanted to know.

"Be honest. Stay out of trouble. Keep the Sabbath holy." Father stopped to take a breath.

John's face turned red. He glanced at his sister, as if asking whether Father knew he had played games with John and Francis Billington in a corner on a recent Sabbath when there was nothing to do between the long meetings. Sarah shrugged. She certainly hadn't told, but Father and Mother had a way of knowing things without being told!

"I know God rested on the seventh day," John said. "But Jesus said if a man's sheep falls into a pit on the Sabbath, there is no sin in getting it out."

"This is true." Father's eyes twinkled. "Remember this, though. If the sheep falls into the pit *every* Sabbath, you should either sell the sheep or fill up the pit!"

Sarah and her family laughed at Father's joke.

A short while later, their laughter stopped. William Butten, a young manservant to Dr. Fuller, died. The passengers gathered on deck for a short service. Sarah huddled between her parents, with John on Father's other side.

This second burial at sea was far different than the first. Few people had mourned the loss of the sailor who had been an enemy of the Pilgrims. Most watched with dry eyes when the man's body was committed to the watery depths. Now a pleasant young man's dream of one day living in the New World had been cut short.

Sarah took a deep breath and listened to Elder Brewster. "It is so sad," she whispered to John after the service. "We don't know if he has any family. William Bradford said he didn't think so." Her voice trembled.

"I know." John looked solemn. Sarah had the feeling he was remembering, as she did, what Father had told them about being ready to die by living right.

The very next day, pieces of driftwood appeared on the water. Birds slowly circled above the ship. Captain Jones cautiously announced, "Smell the change in the air? Notice how the wind has lessened? We must be getting close to land!"

CHAPTER 14

"Land, Ho!"

With the change in the weather, hope again returned to the travelers. All day Wednesday and Thursday the winds decreased. The ship inched forward. Weary passengers slept uneasily, waking now and then to wonder if the storms would come again. So many times when they thought the wind moved on, even worse gales had attacked the *Mayflower.* Would it happen once more?

Daylight came slowly that Friday morning, sixty-six days after the gallant ship had sailed from England. What would the new day bring? Would they really see land, or would Captain Jones's cautious predictions prove to be a false alarm? Sarah and her family roused to a long-awaited call from the lookout, the call even John had begun to think might never come.

"Land, ho!" the lookout bellowed.

Scrambling from every corner of the ship, the passengers raced to the top deck. They peered over the ocean to the western horizon. A low, dim mass showed dark in the chilly November morning. People rubbed their eyes to make sure the thin hump was real.

They sailed closer. A bleak and sandy shore with a few trees appeared.

"Land!" Sarah screamed.

"Land!" a hundred throats echoed her grateful cry.

Elder Brewster's voice rose above the rest. "Praise be to Almighty God! We have reached the New World!"

After her first glimpse of America, Sarah looked away and let her gaze travel over her fellow passengers. Father and Mother stood silently, not cheering like many of the others. John's eyes gleamed, but he kept silent. Tears streamed down worn faces. All turned toward the dim outline that meant the end of their journey. Men as well as women wept and were not ashamed. Many fell on their knees and blessed the God of heaven who had brought them safely to their new home.

Sarah's tender heart filled with sympathy for frail Dorothy Bradford, who lay in her husband's arms, too weak to stand. Stephen and Elizabeth Hopkins were nearby—Oceanus in his mother's arms, their other three children pressed close to their sides. Myles Standish touched his sword. Was he thinking of possible trouble with the Indians? Sarah pulled her shawl closer and shuddered.

Even the Billington boys stood motionless. Sarah grinned. The strong clutch of John Billington's hands on his sons' shoulders showed he had taken to heart Captain Jones's orders concerning Francis and John Jr.

"We are here," John Alden said.

Sarah smiled when Priscilla Mullins raised her head and repeated, "Yes. We are here." A crystal tear slid from one eye, and the look she gave the young cooper said far more than words.

Sarah turned her face back toward land. Bitter disappointment shot through her. Where were the fertile fields in which crops so miraculously grew? Where were the forests that held deer and wild boar for the taking? Most of all, where were the buildings, the homes of those who had come before and sent back such glowing reports?

A little distance away, Klaus leaned against the rail. Now that the *Mayflower* no longer pitched and rolled, Sarah dared go over to him. "Are you glad we are here?" she asked.

"Aye, lass." For once, Klaus made no attempt to scowl and act unfriendly. "I be thinkin' 'tis been a hard journey." His face settled into its usual frown.

Sarah realized how much she was going to miss the crusty seaman. "I suppose you'll be going back soon. To England, I mean. Father said the *Mayflower* would sail back as soon as she was loaded with cargo."

Klaus snorted. "An' where'll we be gettin' cargo?"

Sarah's eyes widened. "Why, from the Virginia colonists, of course."

John's voice cut in. "This isn't Virginia, Sarah." He sounded strange.

"Where are we, then?" She strained her eyes again, hoping against hope to discover all the wonderful things the New World was supposed to have. Her spirits dropped even farther. Not a ray of light came from shore. No ships lay between them and the land toward which they sailed. No activity hinted there were signs of life in the lonely stretch of earth ahead.

"New England," Klaus grunted. "The winds o' fate blew us off course."

"That's right," John said. "Shoals and winds have forced us away from the Virginia Colony where we agreed to settle."

"Oh, dear!" Sarah had counted on warm greetings, perhaps a feast, from those already in the New World. Surely they would be glad to see new settlers, even those who planned to start their own colony. "Now what will we do?"

Captain Jones, John Carver, and others were already discussing the issue. "We have a fine day ahead of us. The wind is slight and from the northeast," Captain Jones said. "We must tack about and sail southward. Agreed?"

"Agreed," the leaders answered. At the captain's command, the *Mayflower* turned and started south. Within a few hours, she reached Pollock Rip, below Monomoy Island, known for heavy breakers and dangerous shoals. Captain Jones eyed it with alarm. Did he dare try to navigate the churning sea, now that the wind had died down?

"We will turn back," he decided. "Nightfall must not catch us here."

"Good thing," John whispered to Sarah. "Klaus says this must be one of the most dangerous areas on the whole coast."

The *Mayflower* finally pulled free of the rip. She slowly sailed north, following the low and wooded shoreline. Before dawn on Saturday, she had reached Cape Cod. The sun rose. The ocean calmed, and the ship sailed into the wonderful, open Provincetown harbor Edward Winslow described as "large enough for a thousand sails to ride in safety."

John and Sarah quietly watched the sails lower. They heard the splash of the anchors drop. The journey had ended. Yet it had taken a terrible toll. Every person showed the strain of hunger and sickness. Even the children had aged in the two endless months at sea.

Behind them lay persecution. Behind lay their friends and loved ones. Were they even at this moment anxiously wondering what had happened to the *Mayflower* and her passengers? Praying, perhaps, that the same God who watched over those in Holland and England might continue His loving care to the Pilgrims?

Ahead lay—what? Winter, cruel and harsh. Fierce storms, too intense for the Pilgrims to search the unknown coast. No friends to welcome them. No towns, houses, or inns to provide comfort. They must continue living on the *Mayflower* until some kind of shelter could be built, and that shelter must be built immediately.

The ship needed to start back to England as soon as possible. Captain Jones must make sure they carried enough food and drink for those on board, but he could decide to leave at any time. If he did, those remaining in America would be stranded—on their own until another ship arrived.

"Who knows when that might be?" many asked.

"The New World is hideous and empty," Sarah cried. She gazed into the wilderness, wondering about the people and beasts that lived there. Would they attack the colonists who tried to take over their land?

"Summer being done, all things stand upon them with a weather-beaten face," William Bradford murmured. "The whole country, full of woods and thickets, represents a wild and savage hue."

Sarah didn't understand everything he said, but the part about the New World greeting them with a weather-beaten face sank into her mind.

She turned away from the forbidding coast, fancying that it shouted, "Go home, Pilgrims. Go home, Strangers. You don't belong here."

Did John sense how she felt? Perhaps. His rough hand squeezed hers. "It isn't home yet, Sarah, but it will be."

"I just feel like we don't belong anywhere." She sighed. "Not in Holland or England or on the *Mayflower* or here."

"I know, but at least we crossed the ocean safely." He ran one hand through his brown hair until it stood straight up and waved in the breeze. "Don't you think God can take care of us on land as well as at sea? He brought us through some pretty terrible storms!"

William Bradford said much the same thing in a meeting of the Pilgrims and any others who chose to attend. "We shall be sustained by the Spirit of God and His grace," he told the assembled group. "Let us give thanks."

One by one, the Pilgrim leaders prayed. Many voices rose loud and strong, John Carver's and William Brewster's among them. Some spoke in hushed tones, as if the men could not believe they had actually defied wind and wave and come safely into harbor.

"Now that we have thanked God, what shall we do first?" someone asked.

"Wash our clothing!"

The reply brought a storm of laughter, but everyone agreed. Long weeks of wearing the same clothing with no way to keep clean had made the living quarters stink. Everyone looked forward eagerly to when they could go ashore and scrub away the dirt and stench of travel.

Just before dusk that evening, Sarah stole away from the other children who were amusing themselves at a game. She needed to think. Besides, she was tired, so tired her bones hurt. "My heart hurts, too," she whispered.

"Are you all right, Sarah?" John came up to where she stood huddled in her warm cloak, gazing at the unfriendly land that would be their new home.

Instead of answering him directly, she said, "Nothing is like we thought it would be, is it?" She hated the little tremble in her voice but couldn't seem to keep it from coming out along with her question.

"I guess not." John shoved his hands in the pockets of his rough coat. "Of course, this isn't Virginia, but maybe it will be even better." He cocked his head to one side and whistled a lively tune.

"How can it be?" Sarah wanted to know.

"For one thing, there's no one here to tell us what to do. If we had landed in Virginia—"

"I wish we had. At least there are other people there," Sarah protested. "And food. I'm not the only one who is worried. I heard Father tell Mother he didn't know how we could survive. It's far too late to plant and harvest any crops."

"Thanks to the *Speedwell* that didn't!" John laughed.

Sarah knew he was trying to cheer her up and managed a weak smile. "I know. It didn't speed well at all." She glanced over her shoulder, facing east.

"We won't starve," John promised, although how he could say such a thing, Sarah didn't know. "Now, what else is bothering you, little sister?"

"Klaus is going to leave us, and I don't want him to go."

"Not as soon as we might think," John whispered mysteriously. "There is a chance the *Mayflower* won't be able to return to England until spring."

"Did Captain Jones say so?" Sarah demanded.

"No, but Klaus told me the year is getting on so fast it may be too dangerous for the ship to start back. It was a stormy enough crossing, and the weather is getting worse and the gales heavier all the time." John sighed, and his usually laughing mouth set in a straight line. "I wish Klaus would stay here. One or two of the crew have agreed to stay and help with the building, but he just laughed and said he was no landlubber. Oh well. No sense worrying about it until it happens. Anything else bothering you?"

"Yes!" A lump rose to Sarah's throat, making it hard for words to get past. "Being hungry and frightened is bad enough, but. . .but, John, it just isn't fair!"

CHAPTER 15

Spying Again!

John Smythe stared at his sister. "Fair? What isn't fair?"

"William Butten," Sarah said in a small voice. Her freckles stood out more clearly than ever, and her green eyes blinked back tears. "Why did he have to die before he even saw the New World? He was so close!"

"It makes me sad, too." John felt the same way he had when Dr. Fuller's young servant had been lowered into the waves. He stared at the shore. "Elder Brewster says we should give thanks that others of us didn't die. Many crossings lose a lot more than one crew member and one passenger. The storms we went through could have torn the *Mayflower* apart."

"I am thankful." Sarah dashed away tears with the back of her hand. "I just wish it hadn't happened."

John continued to gaze at the wooded area ahead of them. "So do I, but it doesn't help to look back. We're going to be plenty busy getting settled before winter gets any worse." He leaned on the ship's rail, then jerked back. "Even with the ship anchored in calm waters, Klaus still keeps an eye on me," John complained. "He has a way of mysteriously appearing just when I'm thinking about doing something!"

"Good for him," spunky Sarah said. "You need someone who can read your mind and stop you from getting into trouble before it happens."

The corners of John's mouth turned down. "I thought you said I'm better than when we left Holland."

"You are, but that doesn't mean you're perfect," she teased.

"What good does it do to try and be good if people just keep thinking you haven't changed?" He knew he wasn't being fair, but he didn't care. It hurt to think Sarah couldn't see how hard he was trying to be the boy Father and Mother and God wanted. Well, all he could do was work harder.

John's good intentions flew away on the breeze all too soon. It began when the leaders called a meeting in the crowded main room to discuss plans. When the men began to gather, John boldly marched in with them.

"What are you doing here?" someone sneered.

John folded his arms across his chest and drew himself to his full height. "I am very close to being a man. I have a right to be here," he haughtily told them. He then showed the irresistible smile that often got him what he wanted.

This time it didn't work. Loud laughter echoed through the crowd, especially from some of the London Strangers. John saw a sympathetic look on John Alden's face, but Myles Standish and others just scowled. In spite of all John's protests, he was ordered away from the meeting.

Anger filled his heart. How dare they treat him like a child? John flexed his wiry arm and proudly noted a swelling muscle. Had he not been one of the few who remained well for most of the journey? Only the worst storms had laid him low, and then only for a short time.

"I can't bear to miss what they say," he told Sarah. "I won't, either." Hot color flew to his cheeks. "I'm going to find a place to hide so I can see and hear what goes on. Come with me, Sarah. You need to know about our future, too."

His sister shook her head until her dark brown braids flopped up and down. "John Smythe, don't you remember the last time I spied with you? Father and Mother were disappointed in us. I felt terrible."

"This is different," he tried to explain. "I went into the meeting openly and honestly. Is it my fault the men wouldn't let me stay?"

"That doesn't excuse your spying," Sarah flared up. She put her hands on her hips the way she did when most upset with him. "Think what will happen if those same men catch you listening!"

"Father won't let them do anything to me, although *he* might!" John said. "Besides, I'm not going to get caught. Neither will you. Please, Sarah?"

To his amazement, Sarah flatly refused. Sneaking admiration crept into John's heart, along with a little feeling of regret. Way down inside, he had to admit how much he'd always liked being able to lead Sarah—even when it was into little paths of temptation! John quickly pushed away the thought and pleaded with her again to join him. Sarah only shook her head and stood her ground.

"If you haven't learned anything on the voyage, I have," she told him. "I can't stop you from spying, but I don't have to join in. Remember what Father said the other time? Brothers' keepers shouldn't go along with other people when they do things that are wrong." She stuck her freckled nose in the air and marched off.

For a moment John was tempted to give up his spying idea. Then he thought of the rumors about all the exciting things to be discussed. No! He had to be there, to learn for himself what lay ahead.

"Curiosity can't be a sin," he told himself. "Otherwise God wouldn't have made me always wanting to know why."

Perhaps not, but sneaking into a meeting where you aren't wanted and shouldn't be is wrong, his conscience argued.

John let out a great breath of air and half turned to follow his sister. The sound of angry voices stopped him in his tracks. Forgetting all about his conscience, he tiptoed toward the meeting room. The door stood open. The men gathered there were so intent on their argument that no one saw John slide inside.

A quick survey of the crowded room showed a pile of torn sails in the corner, waiting to be mended. A single quick dive put John under them. He held his breath and waited, but no one came to challenge him. Heart pounding like waves against the *Mayflower's* hull, the boy lifted a sail. To his disappointment, all he could see was the backs of men waving their arms as they argued.

John dropped the sail. At least he could hear. He bit his lip when laughter bubbled up and almost out. He hadn't really needed to sneak in and hide. The men's voices were loud enough to be heard halfway back to England!

Snug under the sails, John listened hard. He burned with anger when William Brewster, William Bradford, John Carver, and others spoke of the sponsors' demands. "You remember how they demanded ownership of the homes we build?" they said. "And how we must work for them seven days every week, with no time to attend to our own needs?"

A rumble of agreement went through the assembly. "I remember how we sold tubs of our precious butter to pay the port fees," someone called out. John thought it was Myles Standish.

The arguing went on. "We aren't at our grant and have no legal right here."

"We owe nothing to King James! This is the New World, America, a free country. We shall go where we please and do as we choose!"

"Nay," a strong voice protested. "That leads to lawlessness. We must have laws and obey them. We must also stay together. There are few enough of us, God knows. Even with His help, it will take all of us working together to make it through the winter." Someone cheered.

A voice John recognized as belonging to one of the Strangers disagreed. "We who are not of your faith know what will happen. You Pilgrims will take over and force us to obey whatever you decide."

"We shall never do that!" Elder Brewster's clear tones brought a hush to the noisy crowd. "Did we not come to America to get away from the absolute rule of a king? We must make laws and choose the leaders who rule this new land in the same way we choose our church leaders. Every man who is the head of a household shall vote, in order to have a say in the government. What affects one affects our common good."

A little wave of approval sounded from the listening men.

"Write down all our ideas, that we may agree or disagree with them," came the suggestion. "Here is paper. Put on it those things needed to make us a strong colony, one that rules itself."

It took time to list the ideas, to agree even on what would be put down. John grew restless. He wished they would hurry and finish so he could tell Sarah everything he had heard. Even though she would not join his spying, he knew she wanted to hear what had happened.

At last the agreement was reached and signed. It began by saying, "In the name of God, Amen. We whose names are underwritten, the loyal subjects of our dread sovereign King James, by the grace of God, of Great Britain, France, and Ireland, king, defender of the faith. . ."

Questions filled John's mind. Why must they declare loyalty to someone who had treated them so badly?

The agreement went on to state that the travelers had undertaken their voyage to plant the first colony in northern Virginia for the glory of God, the advancement of the Christian faith, and the honor of the king and country.

Again John was confused. How could one honor a man, even a king, so wicked that he executed those who worshiped according to their consciences? John liked the final part of the agreement better. Those who signed it bound themselves to become a body to make fair laws and choose their own leaders as needed for the general good of the new colony. They agreed to obey the will of the majority and vote for rules and leaders.

Make their own laws? Not wait for King James to tell them what to do? Crouched beneath the sails, John covered his mouth with his hands to hold back a cry of excitement. Never before had English colonists broken free from their king's rule! King James always appointed a governor, made rules, and forced the colonists to obey without question, just as they had done in England.

Now the people were free. For the first time in the history of the world, English men, women, and children would live under rules of their own making, rather than the king's.

John could not bear to miss seeing the men sign the paper. He crawled from his hiding place, taking advantage of the excitement in the room, and cautiously worked his way to just inside the door. Should anyone notice him, they would think he'd been drawn in by curiosity. John grinned mischievously. So he had!

The cheering had long since given way to the seriousness of the moment. On tiptoe, neck craned, John watched the men sign, forty-one in all. Though young, they looked old from the hardships they'd faced during the ocean crossing. First to sign the paper was highly respected, godly John Carver, who had been given authority over the trip when the *Mayflower* sailed from Southampton. William Bradford, Edward Winslow, William Brewster, and Isaac Collins followed. Then Myles Standish strode forward, sword hanging at his side. Next came John Alden. One by one the men signed, heads up, shoulders back.

The colonists took their first action by voting John Carver to continue as governor for a year. If he did not do a good job, someone else would be elected to replace him.

John slipped out. His eyes burned. His mouth felt dry—more from the thrilling events he had seen than from thirst. He raced down the deck and waved to Klaus, who gave his usual grunt, followed by a twitch of his lips.

"Sarah?" Words spilled out like beads from a broken string when John found her. He poured into her eager ears everything he could remember and triumphantly ended, "And our own John Carver will continue to be our governor!"

She clapped her hands. The kindly man never failed to stop and talk with the children, no matter how busy he might be with the affairs of the colonists. When John repeated, "We are truly free, Sarah," her face broke into a wide smile.

Later that day, the Smythe family drew apart from the others. Father looked straight at John. "I fear I should punish you severely for spying again."

John's heart leaped to his throat. He felt glad for the early evening shadows that partly hid his face. How had Father known? John cast a quick glance at Sarah, but she shook her head. Good old Sarah! She hadn't told. Thankfulness ran over him. She never would, even though she no longer would let him lead her into mischief.

"What do you have to say for yourself?" Father sternly demanded.

A hundred thoughts chased through John's mind. He would not lie. God surely hated a coward, who refused to accept punishment when he sinned. John looked into his father's face.

"I know I did wrong. I deserve whatever punishment you give me."

He spread his hands wide, unable to put what being there at the signing of the agreement meant to him. "I am sorry to have troubled you, but I cannot say I am sorry for hiding and listening." He looked down.

"For this time *and this time only*," Father quietly said, "I am glad you followed curiosity's leading. I would not have had you miss those moments. They will affect life in America for as long as the world stands!"

John's mouth fell open in astonishment. Sarah gave a surprised squeak. Mother sturdily said, "As am I. None present on the *Mayflower* will forget this day." She laid one hand on her son's rough hair. "My son, your father and I have seen how hard you struggle to be obedient. So has your heavenly Father. Continue trying, John. A man who cannot control himself is only half a man." She and Father moved away together, leaving the children alone.

Two Pilgrims slowly walked by. Their voices sounded hushed in the growing dusk. "Our new colony is to be called Plymouth," one said.

"Aye, and we are pioneers. Along with crops, we plant the light of God's truth in this land to which He has brought us." They passed on.

"Pioneers." John thrilled at the word. "Mother was right. If we live to be older than Methuselah, we will never forget this day. Soon we will go ashore." He fell to dreaming of forests and Indians, wild game and tall grass.

A small hand slipped inside John's larger one. He looked at his sister's troubled face. Sarah had grown braver and more independent during the hard journey, but she was still the little sister who loved and needed him.

Mother's words from what felt like a lifetime ago came back to John. *Deal gently with her.* He freed his hand and dropped an arm around her shoulder. "Don't worry, Sarah. God helped us escape to a free country. He will take care of you." He added, "So will I."

Sarah relaxed. "I know."

John squeezed her shoulder and proudly raised his head. He gazed at the unexplored shores of the New World and silently vowed, *God, no matter what happens, I will keep that promise.* Then he gently led his sister from the dark deck toward the flicker of light below. Father and Mother would be waiting. He grinned. A glint of mischief came to his eyes. So was the New World. He could hardly wait for tomorrow!

If you enjoyed

Sarah's New World

be sure to read other

SISTERS IN TIME

books from BARBOUR PUBLISHING

- Perfect for Girls Ages Eight to Twelve

- History and Faith in Intriguing Stories

- Lead Character Overcomes Personal Challenge

- Covers Seventeenth to Twentieth Centuries

- Collectible Series of Titles

6" x 8 ¼" / Paperback / 144 pages / $3.97

AVAILABLE WHEREVER CHRISTIAN BOOKS ARE SOLD.